DINAANE

Other titles in the series

Afsaneh: Short Stories by Iranian Women
Galpa: Short Stories by Women from Bangladesh
Hikayat: Short Stories by Lebanese Women
Kahani: Short Stories by Pakistani Women
Katha: Short Stories by Indian Women
Povídky: Short Stories by Czech Women
Qissat: Short Stories by Palestinian Women
Scéalta: Short Stories by Irish Women

DINAANE

SHORT STORIES BY SOUTH AFRICAN WOMEN

Edited by
Maggie Davey

TELEGRAM
London San Francisco Beirut

ISBN: 978-1-84659-031-3

copyright ©.Maggie Davey, 2007
Copyright for individual stories rests with the authors and translators

This edition published 2007 by Telegram Books

All rights reserved. No part of this book may be reproduced or transmitted in any form or by any means, electronic or mechanical, including photocopying, recording or by any information storage and retrieval system, without permission in writing from the publisher.

This book is sold subject to the condition that it shall not, by way of trade or otherwise, be lent, re-sold, hired out, or otherwise circulated without the publisher's prior consent in any form of binding or cover other than that in which it is published and without a similar condition including this condition being imposed on the subsequent purchaser.

A full CIP record for this book is available from the British Library.
A full CIP record for this book is available from the Library of Congress.

Manufactured in Lebanon

TELEGRAM
26 Westbourne Grove, London W2 5RH
825 Page Street, Suite 203, Berkeley, California 94710
Tabet Building, Mneimneh Street, Hamra, Beirut
www.telegrambooks.com

Contents

Maggie Davey, *Introduction* — 7

Anne Schuster, *In a State of Emergency* — 9

Alexandra Dodd, *The Transition* — 13

Colleen Higgs, *Looking for Trouble* — 20

Joanne Fedler, *A Simple Exchange of Niceties* — 31

Henrietta Rose-Innes, *Forensic* — 39

Kirsten Miller, *Chance Encounter* — 48

Muthal Naidoo, *The Bridge-Playing Rain Queens* — 57

Mary Watson Seoighe, *The Lilitree* — 63

Willemien de Villiers, *Coming in to Land* — 70

Amanda Gersh, *Home Helper* — 74

Makhosazana Xaba, *Running* — 106

Biographical Notes — 123

Maggie Davey

Introduction

The South African short story was invented by Bessie Head or Herman Charles Bosman, or Miriam Tladi or Nadine Gordimer – or in the reclaimed sand of Mitchells Plain, or was it in the dry hinterland, or in exile or 'back home', or was it 'back in the day', or was it in the throats of the !Xam, or on the wet slasto alongside a pinched swimming pool where the maid slipped or the madam slipped up with the gardener; and then it was between the rounds of buckshot and the sounds of a shot blesbok on a dark farm that called to mind the kicked-up dust of a hundred hooves and the dust-up at Mafeking, of which Solomon Plaatjie wrote in 'A Black Man's View of a White Man's War', when Winston Churchill was still able to run and when the hamstrung Communists were recalled to Moscow and a sangoma purged an illness from a young girl, whose mother knew another and another?

Which is to say that a collection of this nature is a snapshot, a moment, of stories that might catch your eye and hold your ear. Moreover, a woman's moment.

Muthal Naidoo's pensioners in 'The Bridge-Playing Rain Queens' live in a fertile land, where ancient cycads grow and lend their name to the area – Cycadia. Arcadian and pedestrian at the same time, this wet place is reigned over by the delightful Ordinary Rain Queen, (ORQ). The shifting landscape of these short stories gives way to the dry bureaucratic landscape of Lusaka, just prior to the return of the ANC exiles in the early 1990s. In Makhosazana Xaba's story, women are preparing themselves for freedom, but getting bogged down in clauses, while the narrator escapes into a fantasy that is both harrowing and homesick and unfree. Some writers have written the landscape from the air – Willemien de Villiers's character circles over the big hole at Kimberley, waiting to land – and others are back firmly on the ground, as in Mary Watson Seoighe's 'The Lilitree', where a fantastical tree takes root in the Cape. And parkland and park benches and South African suburbia are scenes of difficult decisions, as with Joanne Fedler's shoplifter woman. Alex Dodd's teenage girl narrator feels the pull of the powerful Umgeni River as it passes through her neighbourhood, tamed for a short time, as the character's emotions appear to be. The action in Henrietta Rose-Innes's 'Forensic' unfolds in a park, the scene of a murder, the isolated landscape of sensation and desensitisation. In Kirsten Miller's 'Chance Encounter', the complex story of the drying up of a writer's inspiration is simply told, the landscape all the time in the shadow of an urban drizzle. Landscape and climate, the political versions of weather, historical or current, apolitical or steeped in dank guilt, are evident throughout. Anne Schuster's protestor squares up against the apartheid state in a line of Black Sash women, willingly silent, until further layers of inequality silence her found voice. In Amanda Gersh's 'Home Helper', the comic and utterly sad voice of Julie, a girl scout in the comfortable Cape Town suburbs, listing her needs, but then needing her lists to impress her family and the ubiquitous Brown Owl, delivers an impressive turn as the indomitable Baden-Powell – the little scout, as a little scout for the empire.

Anne Schuster

In a State of Emergency

I read the notice on the back of my placard. Things I can and cannot do. What to do if approached by the police. What to do and say if arrested. Instructions and advice from my organisation in terms of the dictates of this 1987 state of emergency. *Protests must be single. Protests must be silent – refuse to speak to anyone who approaches you.* All very organised and within the law. But really only my white skin protects me. And my white confidence.

I stand in position on the pavement, holding my placard up to the on-coming early-morning rush hour traffic. It reads: 'TO END VIOLENCE, STRUGGLE FOR JUSTICE'. I look into each car as it passes. Most people glance at the sign ... what is it? ... what is she? ... then they look away quickly, and deliberately stare hard at something far ahead in the road. It's a new feeling for me and, I realise, quite a freedom. All these men unable to look at me. All these men I can look in the face without getting a leer in return. Even the aggressive hand-signs and shouts are far easier to receive than my regular daily dose of leers. A crazy thought for women who find the strain of being a constant on-display sex object getting them down – take a break, walk around with a political placard and have a leer-free day!

The women also mostly look away. There are a few who smile, hoot and give a thumbs-up sign. Gives me a full five-minute lift. And the odd black salute. An acknowledgement. To be allowed into the struggle. I'm embarrassed at how much pleasure it gives me. Yes, lady, white lady, your standing there is part of the struggle for justice and might well help to end violence.

It's the first time I'm standing here, in Kalk Bay, my home territory. I usually stand in Muizenberg. Almost like a foreign town there. They don't know me. Here I know everyone. They all know me. Already two of my regular early-morning swimming acquaintances have passed me with a surprised good morning and a knowing look at each other. They are locals – women from the little residential hotel, who float in their bathing caps in the middle of the tidal pool and shout the daily gossip to each other every morning. Somehow I always seem to get them at the beginning or end of my swim.

And here comes that violator of personal space – a round old man in a red bathrobe and slippers. Wherever I happen to sit on the rocks around the tidal pool, he takes off his bathrobe and slippers right next to me and engages in discussions about the coldness of the water today and whether it will be warmer tomorrow and how did I find it today? He is walking towards me now. I can see he intends saying something to me. Last time I saw a woman approach me with that look, she told me how stupid I looked and she wished I would stop a bullet. I was so surprised. I wonder if he will be rude or try to have an argument. I'm glad I'm not allowed to answer. But – he smiles – 'Keep up the good work.' I feel as if I've just been handed a copy of the complete works of Shakespeare by the headmaster at a school prize-giving.

Oh dear. Here staggers one of the local drunks. He looks bad today, teetering on the edge of the pavement holding on to his life and the telephone pole. He looks like he constantly wants to cross the road, standing as if the end of the pavement is a tightrope. His arms swing wildly and then luckily his knees buckle and he sits heavily in the gutter just as a stream of cars goes by. I hope one of his buddies comes along soon and helps him. I'd hate to be standing here struggling for justice while he staggers across the road and gets knocked down by a truck.

I think he has seen me. Probably recognises me as the reliable soft touch for his 'ten cents, madam'. Yes, he does seem to be making his way indirectly towards me. Well, he can see I have no money on me. He weaves right up to me. Another violator of personal space. He breathes in my face, and on my early morning stomach! I step back. He reads my placard aloud to himself. Halfway through, his knees buckle again and he sits on the pavement and continues.

'To end vi- vi- violence ... ssssstruggle for ....'

He looks at me. I look away.

'Jus- jus- justice ...,' he says sitting on the ground. He reads it again to himself, weaving through the words. Then he staggers to his feet and looks in my face.

'Wasshit mean? Hey, lady? Wasshit mean?'

'Can't tell you,' I mutter through closed teeth, staring at the oncoming traffic.

'Hey? Hey Wassat lady?'

'I'm not allowed to speak to you,' I say in a firm undertone and adjust my sign.

'It meanssh that? lady? It meanssh you mussent sspeak to me? Why? I'm not drrrunk. Haven't had anything to dddrink today. Is it from the Bible, lady? I know the Bible. I know G-God. I love God. Does G-God say you mussent sspeak to me?'

He wails and sits again on the pavement half crying, half singing some hymn-like song. He has a good voice but with the sobs he sounds like someone dying tragically in an Italian opera. With a final wail his head hits the pavement. He seems to have passed out. Oh, please let him not have passed out.

I have a horrified realisation of what this scene looks like to the oncoming cars. A poor tattered black man lying sprawled out, looking dead, at the feet of a white lady with a sign saying, 'To end violence, struggle for justice'. Oh no. How can I hold on to the seriousness of it all when this is so bizarre? Oh thank goodness, he has started moaning again and now struggles to his knees. He starts to read my sign again.

'Go away,' I say fiercely. 'Please go away.'
'I – I can rread. I'm not sstupid. I'm ssstill learning.' He sings full throat … 'I'm learning to love yeuoooo … learning to love yeuoooo …' His face slobbers towards me.
'Wotssa notice mean, lady?'
'I can't tell you.'
He stares expectantly.
'The police,' I say meaningfully.
He looks shocked.
'The police will come.'
He looks hurt.
'B-but I wasshn't bothering you, lady, juss asked you a quession, and I'm not drrrunk. Please don't call the p-police, lady. I know you, lady, you know me, you won't call the p-police, lady?' He looks pleadingly at me.

And I know what I'm going to do. I tell myself I have to. I look at him and say with the white-madam voice I have somewhere at the back of my cupboard, 'No, no, I won't call the police if you go away right now. Right now.'

'OK, OK, Madam, OK, I'm going. M-meaning no harm, madam, I'm g-going.' His voice is hurt and offended. He staggers away down the road, while I struggle on for justice.

Alexandra Dodd

The Transition

The end of Eden began in a dream. It was dark and hot. I was fourteen years old and it was December. I can always remember the geometry of that house, but never the details. I can't remember the view, or if there was a window in the room.

There was a time when home was a place with an address. All the post arrived there, and the telephone number stayed the same for so long I thought it would never change. I still remember that number: 843-005.

Trees abounded in the suburb where we lived, giant and generous avocado trees; jacarandas with juicy purple petals that squelched under car tyres in the spring. Our house was on the top of a hill, just north of the city, which I could see hugging the shoreline in a great sleepy curve from my bedroom window.

But there were no trees here. This was not my bedroom. This was not my bed. I don't remember the view from the window. I remember only that my body was lying in tune with the river in that bed on the south side of the house, closest to the Umgeni River. The only remarkable thing about that house was that it was close to the bird park. My aunt and uncle had rented it as an interim measure in a time of financial need, which they were praying would be temporary. It's amazing how long temporary can be. My aunt's hair turned grey in that house.

I see the room from above, like a bird – like one of the big grey hadedas that flocked about the banks of the muddy, red Umgeni. Big, hulking African birds they were. Sometimes, when I was alone in the house, I would have conversations with those strange-shaped birds with their big bodies and their long thin beaks. Not many things could make me laugh when I was fourteen. But the hadedas could – just by being there. So awkward and ancient and out of place – like they'd been left behind by the dodos and the dinosaurs.

'Ha-de-dah,' they'd call out in plaintive ribbons of sound.

'Ha-de-dahhhhh,' I'd yell back to them, extended ribs straining against the tight bodice of my new school uniform.

'Ha-de-dahhhh,' they'd reply, loud and wild. 'We're still here. We're still here.'

In the room was the bed in which I had the dream. It was a single bed with brass knobs and a white cotton cover intricately embroidered with petite flower patterns – 'broderie anglaise' they called it in domestic science – pretty and remote now, from a polyester world. My head lay to the east, nearest to the sea – the big, warm, wavy Indian Ocean. I remember the alignment. My body lay on the same longitude as the river, which flows from high up in the Drakensberg Mountains – the holy heights of the ancient green mountains of Zululand to the sea and beyond.

How warm and slightly wet I felt beneath the hot covers. Hot breath and damp nape of neck in the quiet, humid darkness. And that awful aching feeling between my fourteen-year-old thighs – an adolescent ache for all the beyond that lay on the other side of the sea, far, far away. Under the inconstant rhythms of the straggling late night traffic on Umgeni Road, the broken exhaust pipes and sudden angry accelerations, I imagined the flow of the river and beneath it, the constant low hum of earth. I remember what it was like to lie in that bed and dream. Umgeni. Hadeda. *Lala kahle, umfaan. Tula baba, tulantwana. Tula baba, tulantwana.*' Even while dreaming that dream, I knew it was coming true.

I dreamed that my mother was dead and speaking to me from the grave. She looked like herself, but also like a child. In the dream I was hysterical with loss, so empty that not even gravity could hold me. My body kept rising up to the ceiling. And I kept screaming and crying and railing against the injustice of destiny. Begging for somebody to pull me down again. But my screams didn't seem to reach my mother or affect her. She was present, but gone. She just stood there smiling neutrally, as if she was beyond the tragedy of her own death.

When I awoke I tried to forget the dream. It was summer in Durban and I was staying with my aunt and uncle while my parents were away in London on holiday. All the girls in my new standard seven class at Girl's College were in a frenzy about who to take to the end-of-term party. One afternoon, I was sitting in the lounge agonising with my aunt about what I was going to wear, when the phone rang. My aunt answered.

'How's London?' But then after a while, her tone seemed to change slightly. 'Oh, I see ...'. And then she suddenly she seemed jolly again. 'Right. Okay, fine. No problem. Right, I'll pass you on to her then ... It's your father on the phone. He's got some news for you.' I took the receiver.

'Hello, Dad. How's it going over there?'

'Hello, my darling. How are you doing? How did your exams go?'

'I'm not sure yet. We haven't got our marks back. How's London?'

'I can't even describe how beautiful it is. It's even more fabulous than we could have dreamed of. And yesterday, it snowed! You wouldn't believe how brilliant everything looks in the snow.'

'How's Mummy?'

'She's fine.'

'Can I speak to her?'

'Not right now. She's just taken a walk to the shops. But listen, I've got a surprise for you guys. We've decided that we want you two to join us for Christmas.'

'I thought you'd be home by then.'

'Yes, but it's just so beautiful here, we thought we could have our first white Christmas together as a family. So as soon as school is over, you and James are going to be flying over to London to join us.'

'Wow, I don't know what to say. London!'

'Make sure you bring lots of jerseys. It's freezing here.'

Christmas in London. Nothing strange about that, I kept telling myself. Snow and holly and mistletoe. I tried to recall these things from story books and movies. Famous Five and Secret Seven. Yorkshire pudding, mince pies, scarves and mittens. But outside the Umgeni was thick and muddy, the water running feebly down the centre of the riverbed, leaving the banks exposed and red against the golf course's mowed plains of green grass. It was a still, humid Thursday afternoon and I had nobody to take to the end-of-term dance. My friend, Helen, was starting to volunteer her coolly aloof older brothers. Nothing felt right.

The dance came and went like a fever, and one day in mid-December my brother and I were dropped off at Louis Botha International Airport. Nothing international about it in those days. We waved goodbye and were ushered through the gate at departures by an air hostess wearing a blue-and-orange scarf and stuck smile fixed with pink lipstick.

I sucked on a nauseating lime-flavoured Lifesaver for take-off, sticking my tongue through the absence in the centre until it stung with tiny cuts. The whole way through the safety instructions mime I tried to ignore a creeping nausea accompanied by the thought of being aloft and unable to get down from somewhere vast and empty.

What would happen if my father was alone in the arrivals hall when we came through the gate? What if my mother wasn't there? That would be a bad sign. I tried to think of something else. I put on my airline socks with their sleek flying springbok logos and focused on the choice between Chicken à la King and Beef Curry and Rice written in gold cursive on the menu card.

Then, to cancel out the sign, I made a deal with myself. If my father was alone, there was still hope. There had to be another reason for it. But only one. If he was alone, the reason had to be that he had come to collect us in a Rolls-Royce because he wanted to surprise us. So if my father was waiting for us alone at international arrivals, I wouldn't panic. I'd wait until we reached the garage where the car was parked and if there was no Rolls-Royce there, then I'd know for sure. I didn't know where the idea of the Rolls-Royce came from. But I knew for certain that if the Rolls-Royce wasn't there, we were in serious trouble. I couldn't have stacked the odds against myself any higher. I'd never even seen a Rolls-Royce other than in my father's old copies of *Motor Sports* magazine that lay in a slowly ascending pile next to the toilet in the upstairs bathroom at home.

When my brother and I came through the gates at Heathrow my father was waiting alone.

There was no Rolls-Royce in the parking garage.

'What's the matter?' I said to my father whose expression changed suddenly from jaunty to carrying all the sadness of the world in his eyes.

'She's got cancer, hasn't she?'

'How did you know?'

'I don't know. I just knew.'

My brother had always been a bit bewildered by the world, as if being born was too much of a shock. He had difficulty tying his shoelaces and seemed always to be spilling his Fanta on restaurant tablecloths. On family outings he would invariably get lost, or drop his soft-serve ice cream on the sea horse mosaic in the pavement at Nick Steyn's water wonderland. My mother would spit on a paper napkin and wipe the chocolate off of his cheeks. And then there would be tears and it would be time to go home. Even as he grew older, he could never brush his curly blond hair into shape. He would wake up in the morning singing songs that nobody else knew the words to.

But now he was the contained one, strong in his silence and glued to the LCD screen of his electronic game console. Fixated with the small sequentially flashing objects, he tried again and again to beat his own record, as my father and I sat staring out of the rented apartment window onto the skeletons of trees in this strange snow-covered city, leaking arias.

Down the road from the apartment was a Russian restaurant where we went for dinner one night. The table seemed unbalanced. The legs were holding it up fine, but there was a white linen space where my mother should have been. The symmetry had gone out of things. Knives and forks stayed still in the place where she should have been, cold and metallic. Between Russian silences, we reassured each other that we were lucky. 'She's in the best possible hands,' said my father, moving my brother's Fanta glass away from the invisible rim of the hidden place mat. 'What a blessing that we were in London when she found the lump. She's getting the best possible medical attention here.'

We sat there eating our borscht and thinking of nothing but her. Then a string quartet began to play some sad old Russian tunes and the three of us burst out laughing at the same time. We laughed and laughed until we forgot why we'd started. But that cutlery never moved.

Every day we'd drive to the hospital. It was one of the first operations of its kind in the world – 'conservative surgery', they called it. It didn't work.

My mother's struggle lasted for three years. The remission and then the mastectomy. The septic wounds. The chemo. The vicious scars. The inescapable asymmetry. The hair loss. The depression. The hope. The scans. The lump. The op. The courage. The waiting. The check-ups. The treatment. The waiting. The tests. The courage. The vomiting. The bloating. The weakness. The unending hope. Our desperate belief in the face of her great suffering. And then one day it was over and she was gone.

She died on a Thursday morning shortly after my eighteenth birthday. Even the warm waves were still. After we left the hospital on South Beach, my father took the regular route back home. We passed the old run-down hotels on Gillespie Street. Instead of taking the freeway that runs along the edge of the sea, he took the city road that passed the drive-in across the road from the ice-rink and the huge cinema where we'd all seen *Quest for Fire*. We passed the sports stadium and the turn-off to the Lion Match factory. Then there was that mowed green stretch before the Umgeni, where we drove along the edge of the same golf course we'd passed every other day of our lives – as green, quiet and flat as ever. I noticed a black man bumbling in the bushes for a white man's ball. The course was neatly mowed, as it was the day before and the week before. After the golf course we crossed the bridge over the Umgeni River and then I was finished with that dream and everything changed and kept on changing.

Colleen Higgs

Looking for Trouble

To tell the truth, when Patrick hit me that time, in my face, I wasn't surprised. I wasn't exactly expecting it, but I was expecting something, and after that I stopped. This dread that was eating away at me stopped. So that was how I knew it was the thing I'd been expecting. We'd been seeing each other for about a year, in an on-off fashion. Afterwards, I kept thinking I should have known; I should have been able to prevent it from happening.

I met Patrick at a party I only went to by chance. I'd been to an early movie and was meeting Tina at ten, so I was killing time, browsing at Exclusive Books in Rosebank, when I bumped into Chris, whom I hadn't seen for ages, not since third year at Wits. He invited me to the party, and I almost didn't go, but then I decided that I should. I already had this arrangement with Tina to go to a gig at the Market Theatre – she was pissed off with me for not staying for the whole thing. Mahlatini and the Mahotella Queens were playing and some other performers, and it would be a good jorl, dancing and everything. I think Tina was most put out because we went in separate cars; she always had this big issue with driving around alone after dark.

In any case it was me who had the near-hijacking experience. Very damn close. These two young black guys ambled towards my car. I got in and locked the door, thinking to myself all the time that I was being paranoid. Next thing they were grabbing the door handles and shaking the car. I managed to pull off and they banged the window as I did so. All the way to Greenside my heart was pounding, and I was swearing out loud. I hardly paid attention to where I was going.

I got to the party and didn't know anyone except for Chris, who was otherwise occupied. I didn't care. I poured myself a whisky, and was just settling down on the stairs to have a quiet drink, calm my nerves, when Patrick came up to me and before I could stop myself I was telling him what had happened. 'I don't know how come I didn't panic, and didn't stall – my car's such an old skedonk. I was terrified one of them might pull the door off.'

'It's all right. It's over now,' Patrick said, his voice low and soothing.

'The weird thing is I don't think they're really hijackers. They looked too young. Maybe seventeen. I think they spotted me and thought they'd give it a try. Maybe they just thought they'd have it for themselves. The chop shops would laugh if they'd brought my old Escort in. Sorry, I'm raving ... I was late and Tina, my friend, was waiting for me. I just grabbed the first parking space I could find. I forgot it was going to be dark by the time I got back to the car. I don't even know why I came to this party. I hate parties. But I feel I have to go to them, because otherwise ...' I wasn't sure how to finish the sentence without giving myself away. 'Well, otherwise, I'd spend too much time working.'

'Come on, sweetheart, try to stop thinking about it,' he smiled at me, touching my arm gently. I liked it that he called me sweetheart, even though we'd only just met. Tina wouldn't have trusted that about him, but it felt like something I could sink into after my earlier terror.

'Yeah, you're right. I better go. I'm completely whacked.' I put down my empty glass, still crunching the ice. I didn't even say goodbye to Chris because I wasn't sure how I'd drive home if I stayed any longer. We didn't exchange numbers. Afterwards I didn't want to phone Chris, so I just left it at that. But I couldn't get him out of my mind. He was a small man, with dark hair and eyes that twinkled and danced as though he had some private joke that kept him amused. And this gentle solicitous manner. He was in his early forties, almost ten years older than me, which appealed to me as though it was glamorous.

The next time I saw him was a few months later, at one of those dark, boozy Yeoville parties, too many people crammed into a small flat. I'd been invited third hand and, rather than stay in bed reading, I went along. The saving grace of this party was the rooftop, standing up there, looking out at the city lights strung as far as you could see in any direction, and Ponte, the Hillbrow tower soaring higher than the others. I knew it was the best jorl that night because the short black drug dealer who always wore the yellow felt homburg was there, and all the trendiest trendies were there too. I'd been dancing by myself in the lounge. I pretended not to notice when Patrick came up behind me and put his hands on my hips, then slipped them into the back pockets of my jeans. He danced in this way with me for several songs without speaking, turning me and gliding his hands round my waist and back as he did so. It was the only time he ever danced with me, a ploy to get me into bed. We moved to the rooftop, both drinking Black Label from the bottle. He started to kiss my neck and grip my hair firmly but gently. It wasn't long before I left the party in his car and went to his flat. It wasn't something I usually did, but lately I'd found myself behaving more and more recklessly, as though I was looking for trouble.

We started having an affair – it was never 'a relationship', it never felt like it was going anywhere. He was a journalist, a foreign correspondent for Reuters. He had only recently returned to South Africa. Most of the people I knew were teachers or academics like me or worked in NGOs of one kind or another.

His flat was austere, with only one bookcase filled with books by German philosophers and economics books. There were only six or so novels, two by J.M. Coetzee. He had lots of plants on his balcony and a few indoor plants. There were no paintings on the walls, no ornaments, no tsatskes. He had black Venetian blinds at his bedroom window. Minimalist, he called it.

*

My block of flats had been built in the 1930s, a small two-storey block. I knew all the neighbours by sight. The landlady had recently installed a security gate on the front door and at the garage. There was no buzzer. Friends had to phone ahead or stand on the pavement and shout, 'Jenna, Jenna.' I would lean over from my balcony and throw the key down, but mostly I would run downstairs and let them in – the exercise was good for me.

From the beginning, Patrick used to turn up outside my door. 'D'you want to come for a walk?' Sometimes I wouldn't have seen him for weeks, and once it was even a couple of months. He'd suddenly be there, unannounced, smiling. I always agreed to whatever he suggested. Nothing I was busy with seemed important enough not to drop – it was usually writing a paper, or some endless marking. I would grab my coat or a jacket, some money, put on my shoes and go for a swim, a coffee, a drink, supper, whatever it was he offered. I liked those silent drives and walks through Houghton and the Wilds or Delta Park, places I would never go to on my own. They weren't safe. Everyone had stories of muggings, and worse.

Mostly when we spent the night together it would be at his flat. On his futon, with its clean white sheets. No one knows where I am, I would think. He was such a particular man, his cupboards were all neatly arranged. He did all his own cleaning and ironing, very unusual for a white South African man. He didn't even have a char once a week. He'd lived abroad for many years.

Sometimes he would talk, tell me about when he lived in a squat in London or when he drove a taxi in New York. Or what it had been like to be a scholarship boy at Michaelhouse. I listened and didn't say much myself, my own stories and anecdotes stillborn inside me as I listened, fitting myself to him. I kept hoping he would become more predictable, and that I could start to rely on having him in my life. But he made sure it was never like that. He came and went as it suited him, only phoning when he wanted to, returning the messages I left on his pager occasionally. As soon as I found myself getting used to him he would disappear.

I was on edge, passing time, making arrangements with friends that I hoped I would cancel. Mostly I didn't cancel, and would go to the new art movie at Rosebank or whatever I'd planned to do. The movie I'd seen most recently, *The Piano*, unsettled me. It was a vivid nightmare, beautiful yet disturbing. Afterwards Tina and I had a drink at Times Square. I sipped my brandy and hot chocolate, and listened to Tina describe her plans to sell up and go to London. She kept trying to persuade me to give up on him. I would. Till the next time he appeared at my door. All the while a growing unease built up inside me. I knew that something terrible was going to happen. I just didn't know what it was, nor how to stop it. I became obsessed with the Yeoville rapist to the extent that I slept with my windows closed, even on hot nights. I listened at length to all the stories of the rapist that were doing the rounds. Sometimes I'd wake up at two or three in the morning and, convinced there was danger lurking in my flat, I would get up and look into all the rooms, behind the furniture, in my cupboards. When I was satisfied I was alone, I would get back into bed and sleep restlessly.

*

The final showdown happened on a Sunday, after Easter. I walked over to his flat – I remember what I was wearing, a pale blue t-shirt and white cotton shorts, my running shoes. He was sitting in the armchair in his lounge, slumped in a way that made him look even smaller. He looked defeated, but with an odd tension in his body as though he might spring out of the chair and do something unexpected. The chair was a nondescript, navy blue cotton weave chair. I stood looking down at him, quivering with rage and passion, 'You have to stop this ... thing of coming and going as it suits you. Go or stay, but you can't do both. Just stop it.' He sat there, said little, as if he was totally unaffected by what I was saying.

I got so worked up and desperate to get some reaction out of him I swept an African violet in a pot plant off the table next to me.

'My mother gave me that!' he shouted, his jaw tight. The pot was in shards, soil all over the floor, the purple African violet flowers peeking through the debris.

Before I could see what I'd done (it was only later, replaying what had happened, that I saw the pot, the soil, the flowers) he leapt up and hit me. Not once, but three times in the face. I didn't make a sound. I heard bone and cartilage connecting, a sickening sound and then slumped to the floor, blood spewing everywhere, tears streaming down my face. I put my forehead on my arm, and stayed like that until I could stop crying.

After some time he approached me. 'Get away from me. Don't touch me. Don't come near me.'

I remember washing my face, and the red pouring down the drain. So much blood.

He left me to fetch me some clothes – the ones I was wearing were soaked in blood. In that time I phoned Frank, my dearest friend. I knew Frank would just take me in, and make it as alright as it could be. I couldn't face phoning Tina. I was afraid she would blame me because I'd hung in with Patrick, even though they'd both told me he was no good. 'I'll get him to bring me over,' I told Frank. He wrote down Patrick's address in case I didn't get to his place by six. Later I was glad I'd phoned Frank, because some part of me wanted to forgive Patrick and pretend that nothing had happened. I was tempted to crawl into bed with him and have him hold me while I fell asleep. The phone call was a chink of light in my thoughts; I knew Frank was worried about me and would be waiting for me. It forced the next thing to happen, it meant I had to step away from Patrick and his flat, the mess in the lounge; I had to look at myself and see it was over. We'd broken something that could never be fixed. I felt cold and sad.

After Patrick came back from my flat with clean clothes, before he took me to Frank's, we spoke about what had happened. I watched him clean the floor with a cloth, rinsing it in a bucket. *My blood*, I thought.

'I'm so sorry. I don't know what came over me, where this came from. I know you'll never forgive me.' I'd already forgiven him, but I also knew I had to get away from him, even though I wanted to stay.

I should have seen it coming, I kept thinking. *Not straight away, but quite early on, if only I'd been alert, awake to what was going on, I could have recognised the signs. Why wasn't I overwhelmed with the danger signals?*

Like me, Patrick lived in Yeoville. We used to swim together early in the morning before work or on hot afternoons after work at the public pool. I remember a particular day. We had driven across town to Melville for a change. I sat on the concrete steps next to the pool, I'd swum my twenty laps. Patrick was still in the pool, his eyes insect-like in the black goggles. He always swam at least eighty laps. I closed my eyes, lifted my face to the sun. I could hear the shrieks of children amplified by the water. Patrick swam all his laps in the crawl, while I start off in the crawl, switch to breaststroke and finish off with a last lap in butterfly. 'Showing off,' Patrick teased me, more than once. On this day he stopped in his middle lane, a swarm of children in his way. His face was clenched and cross. He looked up, saw me watching him, smiled and waved. I breathed a deep sigh. He shook the water off his body like a dog as he emerged from the pool. I always smiled to see his tiny black Speedo and the easy way he walked around the pool to where I was sitting to pick up his towel.

I leave my towel as close to the metal steps as I can. He wet me as he shook his head. 'Let's go for a drink.'

'OK,' he kissed the back of my sun-warmed neck. I didn't ask him how many laps he swam, even though I wanted to.

*

I spoke to Tina every day from Frank's house. I wouldn't let her come and see me in the first week. 'If only I'd been more like you, stronger and tougher, he wouldn't have done it.'

'That's not true.'

'Isn't it?'

In the days afterwards, I felt as though my mind was working overtime. I couldn't stop thinking about incidents between us that now frightened me, as though I'd only begun to hear the ominous soundtrack that had been playing all along.

I remembered how he chased me with a squashed dead grasshopper, laughing at me. It was a biggish, green, dead one. Dried out. I noticed it lying on the windowsill while we were having breakfast. I wondered how it got there, up to his fifth-floor flat. Patrick came and stood next to me, suddenly grabbing the grasshopper and thrusting it at me. I panicked, screamed. I could feel my heart beating faster and my face flush. I wanted to get away from him and the insect, but I was trapped. I started to cry and sat down on the floor. I told him to fuck off. 'What's wrong with you?' I asked him. He stood there looking at me as though he was blaming me for spoiling his fun.

One night we both nearly got shot as we were walking around Yeoville in the dark. Several shots were fired a few feet away from us. He flung me to the ground on the pavement behind a car. We waited for ten minutes maybe, till the screams had stopped. A man was lying dead in the street. We heard the police sirens approaching and we left the scene. I can't blame him, but that was the kind of thing that seemed to happen when I was with him.

He slapped me once while we were making love or should I say, having sex. He told me 'women like it if you're gentle, then later you can be a bit rough', as though he had let me into a secret. I felt distant from what he had said, unimplicated, as though he wasn't talking about me.

Another time he invited me to supper. When I got there he was already drunk. He almost burnt the panzarotti and the red pepper and tomato sauce he was making. He flew into a rage and threw several of his white dinner plates and the contents of the saucepan onto the kitchen floor. As we drove across town to a restaurant in Melville to make up for the disaster, all I could think of was seeing him on his hands and knees as he cleaned up this white pasta and red sauce all over the floor. He filled a bucket with warm soapy water and a cloth, wiping up the red mess. Rinsing the cloth, wiping until all traces of his violent outburst had been cleaned up. I stood there, watching.

As I drove back to my flat from Frank's place, I wondered *Do all these pieces come from the same jigsaw box?*, I kept thinking. *Was I asking for it?* As though, if I looked at what happened through a different prism, I would get a different answer, discover a different story. Sometimes I wonder if he knocked some sense into me, because I couldn't understand why I had kept going back for more when he didn't treat me right.

Several times I told him, 'You have a pattern of distance after intimacy. This hurts and undermines me. You usually answer your pager, and when you don't I feel frantic and I worry about you, whether you are okay. Leave me alone and stop coming back if you don't want me to worry about you.' Sometimes when I tried to talk to him about what wasn't working for me, it was as though I was hearing a voice-over, as though somebody else was talking and I wasn't even in the room.

A few days before the incident, I was driving down Louis Botha. I spotted his metallic blue Golf parked outside the Radium. I stopped off; he was drinking a beer and watching the cricket,

England playing Pakistan. He bought me a beer and fish and chips, and was pleased to see me. I felt so happy that afternoon, as though I had a real relationship and as though it might all work out after all.

*

I learnt that it takes three weeks for bruises to heal. Later, in a picture Frank took about a month later, we'd gone to the Magaliesberg one Sunday for a picnic and I can still see the ghosts of the bruises. I look like a woman who is tired or is recovering from a life-threatening illness. I start to see other women with bruises. It was not something I'd noticed before. Women of all shapes and sizes and races have bruises on their faces. I recognise their awkwardness and shame. Once or twice I've wanted to say something – but what? *I see you?*

Sometimes I circle back to the bruise Patrick gave me. I think of how as a child I liked bruises, they were badges of honour, something to return to, to contemplate. If you poked them, they would hurt a little, and as the bruise faded and changed colour magically from purple to green, so would the hurting. You could show off bruises to friends, get a cuddle from your mother. It was evidence that you had been hurt, and that you had survived the hurt.

Other hurts, grief, disappointment, betrayal, live in the dark – there's nothing to show, nothing to point to.

Bruises came from falls and bumps, from rushing and climbing and colliding. They were from being busy and alive, from riding bikes, jumping out of trees. I never got a bruise from a person until I was an adult woman. It was not a bruise I was proud of.

One night at Times Square I was wearing a loose white cotton dress and my suede jacket, my legs bare. He was drinking whisky. I loved living in Yeoville, the short walk to Rockey Street. That night we wandered street after street in the dark, admiring the Art Deco features in the lobbies of blocks of flats.

Sometimes I still think about how warm and scented the air was, and how it was an adventure to be making this private inventory of architectural details. No one can take away the past, what people have meant to each other. Sometimes I wonder if he ever thinks of me, if he hates me or is still sorry. We had a sexual magic: does he still think of that? He suffered a public humiliation because of what happened, because of what he did to me. Chris, our mutual friend, told all his friends, his crowd. It was different for me, but all the same it left shame in me, lodged in my body.

I liked it when Patrick had been in my bed. I used to find hairs from his beard on my sheets. Sometimes when you make love with someone, you get hair in your mouth, it's one of those surprising things that no one mentions, not even in books.

I didn't expect to lose him for good. I can't have him back, and none of it has gone away. I still feel the hard pebble of pain, somewhere deep inside. I dream I am a dead woman made of straw who comes to life. I dream my mother gives me a mechanical bull for my birthday. I dream I live in a glass flat in a tall building, and the sun streams into my lounge, until it is too hot.

Joanne Fedler

A Simple Exchange of Niceties

Perhaps the truth depends on a walk around the lake.
Wallace Stevens

The first available appointment was for next week. That was in nine days' time. Enough time for hands, brains, eyelids and knee joints to form, according to the charts. I took a walk. I needed to sit on a bench somewhere under a tree, have a smoke. I know you're not supposed to smoke when you're pregnant, but fuck it, I didn't ask to be, and in nine days' time, it was all going to be scraped out of me anyway which is a lot worse damage than a cigarette.

There is only one bench I like to sit on in the park. It's that one just to the left of the big duck pond. It's got generous slats, not those awkward stingy ones that protrude into your back and don't let you forget you're sitting on public property. I once saw seven black swans there, gliding together; it was like a ballet. It sort of made me cry, I don't know why. Just that perfect connection, unspoken like that. I like benches. They make you feel as if people matter, you know, ordinary people just like you, who haven't achieved much in life, despite all your teenage dreams of Paris and art school. Benches like that don't seem to mind that you've never reached your potential or managed to finish anything you've ever started. They just sit and wait for you, an invitation that's never revoked: come, sit.

I know it's stupid to be possessive about things that don't belong to you, but I like to think of that bench as *my* bench. Put there especially for me, and only for me. You know when you're a little kid and everyone else runs ahead, and you feel like you're going to be left behind? When I get to my bench and it's empty, it's as if I've been waited for. Like an older cousin who stops and holds out a warm friendly hand, not minding being last together with you.

If I arrive at my bench and there's someone else already there, I just walk on. It's not that I don't like sharing. I'd give anyone the shirt off my back, or the food off my plate. That's part of my problem. My parole officer said people take advantage of that sort of thing. Makes them think you're easy. I don't know. I don't like to see people go hungry or to have to sleep in bus-shelters, which are the unfriendliest of public spaces.

I just like to be consulted first..

And if I'm already sitting there and someone comes and sits down without even a simple exchange of niceties, like, 'Do you mind?', 'May I?', 'Do you want to be left alone?', well, that's just bad manners..

Once, when that old lady shuffled up to my bench, I got all panicky. She reminded me of my Nan who's been dead for more than ten years, but who had a soft spot for me, always pressed some cash into my hand, and whispered 'Go buy yourself something nice.'

The old lady smiled and sat down beside me, and fiddled with her plastic bag, which had got stuck on her wrist, twisted around and around. It took her a good few minutes to work out which way it was twisted and how to untwist it and remove it. I tried not to care what it was she had in her plastic bag, but I couldn't help seeing she had shoes in it. A pair of bright red little girl's shoes.

And that was it. She snatched my peace from me.

'It's a cloudy day,' she said. I didn't know whether she was directing it at me, or just like at the water.

I nodded. When I'm sitting on my bench, I'm generally not in the mood for small-talk and chit-chat.

I got up soon after that and left her there, with her little red shoes in her plastic bag.

Today, of all days, I needed to be alone on my bench. I rounded the corner and saw the bench – unoccupied!

I quickened my pace, though there was no one else in sight, just to claim it. I lay down, taking up the entire bench with my body. I reached into my pocket and took out a cigarette. 'Smoking may be dangerous in pregnancy.' I laughed out loud – it was a fucking cigarette that got me into this mess in the first place.

When Damien had approached me at the pool table, and leaned in against me, he said, 'Got a cigarette on that cute bod of yours?'

I liked the confidence and he cut a fine figure in a pair of Levi's.

He fucked me from every direction and on every surface in my apartment. I still have bruises in places I can't see without contorting myself into a yogic position from which I couldn't disentangle myself without professional help.

We hadn't spoken much, so I couldn't have known he didn't want kids. Not with a trashy whore like me – his words. As if a kid was on *my* agenda. I guess I never thought before how those two pink lines kind of make an equal sign to the end of a relationship. 'Better to know someone thinks you're a trashy whore sooner rather than later,' Barbie said. She's my best friend and I swear the greatest hairdresser, which is why I always look good even on a waitress's salary. She gets me right. I heard her. Better to know. Even if you had feelings for that person. Those feelings get the message not to hang around, not after *trashy* and *whore* have been hurled at you like a double fist in the guts. When just two nights before, he held his strong hands behind your hair and licked you from your throat to your bellybutton in a way that made you think, you know, that maybe he loved you.

'Do you mind?'

I looked up.

Did it look like I didn't mind? I was lying down, relaxing on my bench, one hand on my belly, the other holding my cigarette. Clueless, as Barbie would say rolling her eyes.

I swung my legs down and sat up. It made me a bit dizzy.

'You shouldn't smoke,' she said, sitting down.

'Well thanks for your concern,' I said. 'Not like it's any of your business.'

'You're right, it's none of my business,' she said. She opened her bag and took out a bottle of mineral water and took a big glug out of it. What is it with people and bottled water? Like there's something trashy about tap-water.

She was married, or at least she wore what looked like a wedding band on her finger.

She took a book out of her bag and rested it on her knees while she looked out at the lake. '*When fertility fails*' it was called. She flicked it open and started to read.

She caught me looking at the title.

'We've just been told we can't have kids,' she said to me.

I shrugged. 'It's none of my business,' I said.

'Right,' she said.

I sat there next to her inhaling my cigarette. She turned the page eight times. Hell, she could read fast.

I thought maybe I felt something move inside me, but that couldn't be the case. I was only eight weeks pregnant. They only start to move around eighteen or nineteen weeks, that's what that book I paged through at the clinic this morning said. Not that I was interested or anything. It's just that they make you read these things before you can consent to a termination.

As we sat there, a duck swam past.

'I don't want to be an old duck, swimming all on my own,' she said.

I shrugged. 'There are worse things than being on your own,' I said.

'Like what?' she asked.

'Like being with someone who doesn't love you.'

'Children always love their parents,' she said. 'And parents always love their kids.'

'You haven't met my mother,' I said flicking off ash which had dropped on my shirt.

'Of course your mother loves you ...' she said.

'She would have exchanged me for a week's holiday at a three-star resort ... not that anyone was offering ... but if they had ...'

'You're wrong,' she said shaking her head.

'Have it your way,' I said. I swear people who drink mineral water obviously know something I don't.

And then, and I didn't see this coming, or else I would have got up and left the bench much sooner, she started to cry.

'Please don't cry,' I said.

'I'm sorry,' she said. 'I just wanted children so much.'

I sat there, watching her cry. 'Think of all the money you'll save,' I offered.

'We've spent our entire life savings on four IVF treatments,' she kind of snickered. 'And, you know what, I'd sell every single thing I own, just to be a mother ... everything, every heirloom, diamond ring, Persian carpet ... all of it ... it's all worthless.'

I thought about what I could do if I owned diamond rings and Persian carpets.

'It wasn't meant to be,' I found myself saying, which really wasn't me speaking. It was like my Nan just popped out of my mouth.

'Yes ... you're right,' she said turning to look at me. 'It wasn't meant to be.' The tears carried on streaming down her face. She closed her book and put it in her bag.

'I guess I have to get back to work,' she said. 'Thank you for listening ... I'm so sorry to burden you with my problems,' she laughed. 'You must think I'm crazy.'

I shrugged. 'Hell, I've got no certificate in sanity ...'

She got up.

'Do you come here often?' she asked.

I did come often. But not to talk to strangers.

'Maybe I'll see you again,' she said. 'This is my favourite bench in the park. I always think it's been put here specially for me, isn't that silly?'

Look, I've never done anything with my life. The shoplifting thing just kind of happened, which led to the three months inside. My mother wouldn't even put up the $500 bail for me. I guess I understand her point. I'm bad news. I hang around in pubs after work. I'm not going to amount to anything. It's not like I'm going to find a decent bloke and get married. Barbie says I'm like Ruby Tuesday in that Rolling Stones' song. I can't be chained – unless it's for sexual purposes, now and then.

So I had this thought. She seemed so bloody keen on kids. Since I'm already pregnant and all that, maybe I'll just have it, and give it to her. That way, I can get to go and visit the kid now and then without the hassle of having to bring it up myself. It was the first time I ever thought about coincidence and fate and all that stuff; you know, where pieces all just fit together.

The next time I came to my bench, I had just come from the 'half-way' scan. 'It's a little girl,' the doctor said, which I already knew. She liked the same kind of music as me, really got frenetic when I turned up James Blunt on those little headphones I attached to my stomach. At least she'd have good taste in music.

As I looked at the shadows on that fuzzy screen, I didn't feel like such a trashy whore anymore.

Though I waited at my bench for an hour, the lady with the book on fertility didn't come. I wondered what she might call her little girl.

'Summer,' I said out loud. 'That's a good name for a little girl.' I thought I might suggest that to her when I handed the baby over. Kind of like a 'use it, don't use it ...'

The time after that, I really needed to sit down and it was a huge relief to put my feet up and feel the sun warming them. I was retaining water in my legs and it was getting harder to fill my shifts at the restaurant without my back hurting. Also it was getting hotter and my belly was as smooth and ripe as watermelon.

Even Barbie revised her opinion about pregnancy being 'grotesque', and I didn't feel fat, the way I thought I'd feel. And when I told my mother I was pregnant, I guess I didn't foresee that she'd start crying on the phone. Like from happiness.

'I'm not keeping it, Ma,' I told her.

'Don't you DARE give my granddaughter away,' she said.

I never thought of it like that. It gave me a lump in my throat. My mother thought there was something about me worth keeping.

She went and knitted a pink cardigan with rosebuds on it. I kept it. To give to the lady along with the baby, and the name suggestion.

And my mother started sending money in the post each month.

I was never tempted, not even once, to spend it on myself.

By the time Summer came, it wasn't so much that I'd changed my mind. But since she was 'distressed', and nearly choked on her umbilical chord that was wrapped around her little neck, and given that my mother was at my side, holding my hand, and crying, I thought I'd just make sure she was alright for a while. When she fell asleep on my chest with her little hand curled under my chin, mum said to me, 'I remember you lying on my chest like that too and wishing it would never end.'

That's how come I ended up with my mum lying on the hospital bed with me, with my head in her lap, while she stroked my hair, whispering 'beautiful girl.' It was either meant for the baby or for me, but it didn't matter.

I did go back to the bench, with Summer, to look for that lady with the book and the mineral water and the Persian rugs and heirlooms.

I guess if she'd been there, I could have done something really nice and given her the baby.

But my bench was empty.

Henrietta Rose-Innes

Forensic

It was a mistake, coming here. Paula hadn't been to this park since childhood, when it had been a limitless realm; but now she saw that it was small, only about the size of a rugby field, and exposed. There were worn patches in the grass, a brandy bottle in the dry pond that had once held carp. She had hoped the place would feel safe, but instead it was desolate.

The lawn sloped up gently between patches of shrubbery. At the top end, a bank of pine trees separated the park from the reservoir beyond. The sky was pale, full of clear sunlight that reflected off the few white-painted benches. Down near the entrance, a nanny sat with a toddler on a blanket, but otherwise the lawns were empty. A weekday afternoon. Paula wanted to get under the trees, somewhere private and away from the road; but Mariette was dawdling behind, a dark figure afloat against the green.

A mistake. This was not the right place to bring her cousin. The nanny was folding up the blanket now. Soon, Paula realised, she and Mariette would be the only people there.

A guinea-fowl darted between the flowerbeds – a speckled mother followed by a row of droplet chicks. Mariette came up the slope behind the birds and then stopped, arms crossed, waiting.

'Let's go in the shade.' Paula pointed with her free hand. In the other she held the handles of a plastic shopping bag containing four beers. She'd been unsure about the beers. Mariette was only sixteen, four years younger than herself; she didn't want to get her little cousin drunk. Or maybe just slightly. So she'd torn open the six-pack and left two bottles at home. Two each should be fine.

Mariette shrugged. Her shoulders were made for shrugging, angular and mobile beneath the black polo-neck. There was little family resemblance between the cousins, except that both were tall and dark-haired. Mariette had a small square face, neat features, a wiry prettiness that Paula, softer fleshed, had always envied. The younger girl's wavy hair, worn loose down her back, seemed freshly washed. But she was gaunt; the shine of her hair was at odds with the dead surfaces of skin and eyes. She wore a long brown skirt of some silky material, dark stockings and black suede boots with a heel. Clothes to conceal, but tight, their bandaging material exposing the sharpness of knee and elbow. A black satin ribbon was tied like a choker around her neck.

Last time Paula had seen her, a year ago, Mariette had been emphatically made up – Egyptian eyeliner, dark lipstick, hair streaked with red. Then it had seemed childish to Paula, melodramatic; but now she missed the colours. Mariette's naked face was powdery and dry, not the way a young girl's skin was supposed to look. And she had grown so thin that when her arms were tightened across her chest, as now, it looked as if she were binding dark cords around herself. A paperback book was caught in the awkward clinch, pushed into one armpit. She'd squeezed an index finger between the pages to keep her place. It looked painful; Paula could see that the top joint of the finger was white.

Mariette had irritated her in the car, reading all through the silent journey to the park.

Paula headed for the shade of an old rubber tree, Mariette trailing. The grass had worn away to earth around the humped roots.

'How about here?' She dropped the bag of beers on the ground, where the sand was pocked with ant-lion holes like miniature volcanoes. Just beyond the rubber tree, the lawn ended and the wooded bank rose. A narrow path, edged with worn brick, led up into the pines.

Mariette shrugged again, then bent from the waist to help herself to beer. An elegant movement that combined worldliness with years of ballet lessons. When she saw her cousin pop the bottle open with a practised snap of the wrist, Paula knew she should have brought the six-pack after all.

Moving just beyond the tree's shade, Mariette set the bottle down carefully on the uneven grass. That ballerina trick of going from standing to sitting in a single fold. Then she stretched out on her stomach, ankles precisely crossed, as if she'd decided beforehand how to compose her body. Shifting her elbows together, she held the fat paperback open in both hands. It had a red-and-black cover, featuring, as far as Paula could see between Mariette's fingers, a dead hand floating in blood-coloured light.

Paula moved unwillingly out of the shade and sat down cross-legged next to her cousin. 'Detective book?'

'It's about forensic pathology,' Mariette answered in a faint voice.

Paula had read one or two books like that – maggots and blood-spatters and knife-cuts. She could feel her cousin slipping away; she was losing the moment. She must try to say something, now, before Mariette turned another page.

'It's interesting,' Mariette offered unexpectedly. 'I might be a pathologist when I leave school.'

Mariette hadn't been to school since July, Paula's mother had said. Paula shifted her legs, pulling her knees up. Sitting cross-legged made her thighs look fat, and the grass was prickling. She'd considered bringing a blanket, but had decided against it: the crocheted patchwork had seemed old-womanly, fussy. 'Isn't it a bit gross?' she asked. 'Dead bodies, and all that.'

Her cousin gave a cool half-smile, not looking up.

Paula ploughed on. 'I wouldn't want read that kind of stuff. i If I were you.'

Mariette went still. Her eyes did not leave the page, but they no longer scanned the lines. 'What do you mean?'

'Ah, nothing,' Paula flushed, but she was already pink from the sun and perhaps it didn't show. She clenched her toes inside her running shoes. 'You know, violence.'

A small, stern face turned towards Paula. 'Did my mother ask you to talk to me?'

'No – well,' Paula hesitated, 'Actually my mother.'

Mariette was impassive. 'I'm fine,' she said. 'I don't want to talk about it.'

Would she prefer her little cousin to cry? Tears would make this easier, Paula thought.

'Well, if you ever do, you know – '

'Ja.' Mariette closed the book, first carefully folding down a corner of the page to mark her place, and put it to one side on the grass. Then she pulled her legs under her and stood, ankles together, beer in hand.

'I'm going for a walk,' she said, and headed off up the path into the trees, reaching out to strip a leaf off a bush as she went. She walked quickly now, not looking back.

Paula sank back on the grass, cross-legged, reminding herself: patience. Mariette was the damaged one, the one who must be cared for. Paula must be patient, gentle. As if I am ever not, she thought.

She picked up the thick wad of the book and leafed through it – thin, cheap paper. It opened on the page Mariette had marked: *... retracting skin from the cranial ...* Her gaze flicked away from the words. Paula had never had the stomach for this kind of writing; the formalin-soaked relish of it. She always imagined herself the body on the slab, not the steely forensic pathologist with the implements in her gloved hands. She flipped to another page. Now the pathologist was cooking a romantic dinner for two. Paula pushed it away.

The grass was starting to feel like tiny blades, even through Paula's shorts, and she could also feel movement – ants under her legs. Worms. But when she checked she saw nothing, just pink leaf impressions on the soft flesh of her thighs. She moved back into the shade of the tree, idly looking for ants to feed to the ant-lions. But there were none. She sat down and opened another beer.

Mariette stayed away for ten minutes; twenty. The light grew soft, shadows lengthened. It was dim in the trees beyond the lawn.

Look after her Paulie, you know what a bad time she's had. Just take her out for the day, just one day. Talk to her.

We were never that close, Mom.

Mariette had been different, apparently, since July. That's when Aunt Denise had come home to find the house burgled, Mariette unconscious in her room. There'd been terrible bruises on the girl's neck, and perhaps worse, Paula's mother had hinted; Denise had not told all of it. That was four months ago. Mariette herself had said nothing about the incident, not in the hospital nor at any time since. For the first week, she hadn't spoken at all.

What do you mean, close? She's your cousin, Paulie. You used to play together.

Long ago, on the beach. She'd been given her cousin's hand to hold. Mariette was an outgoing, pretty five-year-old, hair in pigtails, wearing pink panties and nothing else. Her small hand was mobile in Paula's. It was an easy accident to happen: the energetic little girl had squirmed from her grip and run towards the shallows, and Paula had felt incapable of stopping the child, of preventing her disappearing into the waves like a mechanical toy wound up and released. Paula had not taken a single step towards the water.

The undertow had grabbed Mariette by the ankles and tipped her so her head went under, stayed under for thirty seconds or more. Only then did Paula shout. Aunt Denise had rushed forward to grab the little girl by an arm and an leg and lift her clear, turning in the next moment to stare with terrible accusation at the lumplike nine-year-old standing on the shore.

They'd pressed at Mariette's white chest with their hands and she'd puked up water and thin bile and then started coughing, staring not at her mother between coughs but fiercely up at the sky. Afterwards, wrapped in a towel on the back seat next to Paula, Mariette had seemed tired but pleased. *What a brave girl*, Paula's mother had said. Not looking at Paula.

Eleven years later, Paula could still feel the shame, but also the odd disappointment she'd experienced. There had been, for a few short moments, a simple curiosity; a desire to watch what happened when the child's clockwork legs carried her into the sea. As if Mariette were a little machine that Paula had devised in order to test something she was afraid to try for herself.

'Hey!' The shout was piercing, so buoyant that Paula didn't immediately recognise the voice. Then Mariette came running down the path, laughing like a child, and Paula started to laugh too, feeling that some kind of breakthrough had most unexpectedly occurred. She almost opened her arms to embrace her cousin – it felt that natural.

As Mariette got closer, Paula saw the flush in her cheeks. She was shouting. 'It's a man! I found a man!'

Mariette came up to her, closer than they'd been all day. Her whole posture had changed – now not primly upright, but leaning forward, eagerly taking hold of Paula's arm with both hands. Her grip was strong.

'What?'

'There's a man in the bushes. A dead man.'

The sunlight was cold. A guinea-fowl gave its rusty-swing call somewhere lower down the sloping lawn and Paula was startled, almost as if the creak of dismay had come from her own throat.

'Come see, come *see*.' Mariette was turning, pulling at her arm. Long strands of dark hair were twisted around her neck.

The path tilted up through the trees, away from the sunny lawns and into shadow. Paula resisted the tug. 'Mariette ... are you sure?'

Mariette's face snapped shut again. She snatched her hand

away, then turned and stalked up the slope, grace lost, with the stiff determined gait of a child heading for the waves.

And so Paula followed, in under the pines, into the damp shadows where the light failed. She watched Mariette's white hands swinging at the ends of her black sleeves, disconnected from her body in the gloom. The path looped back down, but Mariette plunged off it, straight up the steep trackless slope. Thick undergrowth grew here, and Paula felt the branches scratching blood from her hands as she pressed her way through. She moaned softly to herself. Then the slope flattened out and she came up with relief against a fence; Mariette was waiting, gripping the wire. Paula stopped, breathing through her nose to conceal her panting. She gave a little laugh, to show that she didn't blame Mariette for teasing.

But then Mariette hitched up her skirt – a line of pale, sinewy leg – grabbed the wooden fencepost and climbed over, nimble in her heeled boots.

Paula didn't bother to protest. With difficulty, she followed; she was not agile, and the toes of her running shoes were too snub to fit the diamond gaps in the wire. She teetered on top, the fence rocking under her, thinking for an awful moment that she would fall with a leg on each side. But she made it over.

Mariette had broken through the bushes into a small clearing where the sunlight fell onto rubble – bricks, rusty cans and broken glass, knit together with grass. On the other side, the bushes pressed thickly against another fence, then more trees; beyond, a glint of water from the reservoir.

Mariette was pointing at a tangle of old rubbish. Her empty beer bottle stood to one side. 'There!'

'I can't see anything, Mariette,' Paula said in a calming tone, still trying to control her breathing.

'*Look.*'

Paula stared. Then slowly, transmuted by Mariette's pointing finger, the pile of rags took form. A blue anorak. A pair of shoes. A bundle of yellow-grey sticks, loosely threaded through the bright, imperishable synthetics, grass pushing up between them. Then Paula made out a yellow skull, staring straight up, the jaw still attached by leathery shreds; hands twisting out of the blue sleeves, skin peeling back from the delicate bones of the hands like dry leaves curling ...

How lonely, was Paula's first thought. She felt no revulsion. There was no smell. It was dry and unfrightening. She noted the cheap fabric of the clothes, the worn soles of the shoes. Poor man's clothes. The body had been there a long time – months, years. How could it have passed through all the garish stages of death, unwitnessed? To reach this state of quietude. Paula moved towards the body, feeling some need to cover it: shut up the eye sockets, fold the arms and legs, zip the sad anorak; something.

'Don't go too close,' Mariette said sharply. 'It's evidence.' She was talking swiftly, intently. Her hands were on her hips, not tucked up into her armpits now. 'They need to bring the forensics team in here as soon as possible, cordon off the scene.' Mariette's eyes were bright as she lifted her hair away from her neck and twisted it up with both hands, giving her flushed neck some air. 'It's a man, don't you think? Must be a man,' she said, shaking her hair loose again. 'I've always wondered what it'd be like to find a body.'

Paula didn't watch them gather up the remains. When she saw them carrying the narrow bundle on a stretcher down to the road where the mortuary van was parked, she thought they treated it roughly and without care.

But the policeman was gentle. The large man sat next to Mariette on a white bench next to the park entrance and took her statement, pressing on his knees. The ballpoint pen kept pushing holes in the paper, and Paula worried about him getting ink on his trousers. His uniform was immaculate. An enamel nametag said *MAJOLA*.

Mariette, next to him, was straight-backed again, her hands on her own sharp knees, staring ahead and talking with quick animation.

'It was a man, I could see at once it was a man. And of course I knew it wasn't a natural death,' she was saying. 'From the position of the body. There'd been a struggle. Abrasions, bruising on the neck. And cuts, knife-cuts – all over.' Her voice was trembling now, tissue paper floating above a fire, on the edge of combustion. 'The blood had ... *pooled* around the body.'

The policeman raised soft, puzzled eyes. 'Blood? Where's the blood?'

Paula started shaking her head, but he wasn't looking at her.

'A blade with a thin cross-section,' Mariette continued. 'But cause of death was strangulation. Fractured hyoid bone. Classic.'

Sergeant Majola had stopped writing now and was staring blankly at Mariette.

'Excuse me,' said Paula. She motioned the policeman away, and he stood and walked with her a little way up the lawn. Mariette stayed on the bench, staring bright-faced into the setting sun.

'My cousin is upset,' said Paula. 'We didn't go that close. There was no blood or anything. Just what you saw. That's all.'

In the car on the way home, Mariette's long hands came up to the ribbon at her neck, fingertips together and palms facing out, an inside-out prayer. 'A horrible way to die,' she said thoughtfully.

'Yes.'

'I wouldn't want to go that way.'

'No.' Paula shifted her eyes sideways, and saw that her cousin had undone the ribbon, was rubbing the silky stuff between her fingers. Her neck was unmarked.

'Your book, we left your book behind,' Paula remembered.

Mariette gave a secret smile. 'That's okay,' she said. 'It wasn't such a good one anyway.'

She rolled down the window a crack and trailed the ribbon out of the car. It fluttered for a moment, a strand of seaweed in the flow, then whipped away behind them as she let it loose.

KIRSTEN MILLER

Chance Encounter

It's been done before, this meeting of the self on a lonely road. It's not an original idea, just as there's nothing about my life that is novel or new. I am another like thousands before me, thirty-five, married, no kids – nothing special.

I walk, this evening, to the local garage as the sun sinks behind the suburb and the rain subsides. I walk in the wet along a busy main road and I cross at the place where I can see furthest in both directions, from the painted yellow island that divides the road in two. I walk and I feel urban, like I'm part of the street in my stone Cargo trousers and neutral t-shirt, like I blend in because I'm not stuck in the capsule of a luxury vehicle with two point two kids sitting in the seat behind me. I'm not judging them, those suburban women who ferry their offspring around from baseball practice to ballet; it's just that I feel incredibly different from anyone else that I know.

Call it loneliness, lack of sociability, downright eccentricity; it's taken on different forms in my life and what I now know is that it's not going away. I've always craved solitude. I'll walk for miles given half a chance, and not to anywhere or for anything but just to walk, because the rhythm itself creates a kind of trance, and that's how I feel when I walk, as though I'm not quite of the world, but I'm still in it.

My oldest friend is in town, just for one night. She's passing through on the way to Joburg and she called me today, to see if we could hook up. I lied to her. I told her I was working late, that I had meetings until six o'clock that might go on till seven. It's my craving for solitude. I don't have the energy to drive any more than I have to, anywhere further than I have to go. I don't want people. I don't want things to do or conversations that go nowhere in particular. I just want to walk, to feel the rain on my face; I just want to be alone.

It began in London, when I lived there long ago. I lost myself in that city, walking until I was delirious and then returning home eventually to scribble my fragments of thoughts into scrappy notebooks. I still walk, but I stopped the scribbling years ago. The notebooks piled up, and eventually I banished them to the back of my cupboard when I failed to find anything meaningful in them that might take me forward.

I pass the taxi rank and feel the eyes upon me. When I was new in this neighbourhood I crossed the road before I reached this point, uncomfortable as the only white face in a sea of people who looked at me as the odd one and wondered what I was doing walking amongst them. Now I walk through the crowds as they wait for commuter transport to ferry them home or wherever else they want to go; some eyes are hostile, some mouths greet me, others simply watch me with curiosity. I wonder what I look like to them, a lonely white woman with a cap on her head and her hands in her pockets, tramping the streets alone. Past the taxi rank and under the bridge, the roar of traffic above me on the highway. Here most of all I feel a part of the street, like I could blend into the concrete and never be found again. My body aches like I can imagine what it's like to be eighty, and yet walking makes me rise above it, the motion takes me away from myself.

At the end of the road I turn left and into the petrol station with its rows of pumps and sullen attendants who would prefer to sit and gossip than serve their customers. I go into the shop and purchase two loose cigarettes and a box of matches. It's an easy transaction, a familiar one, and it carries less guilt than the boxes of smokes I used to buy. 'Two loose, please.' It's a daily phrase that rolls off my tongue as though it's an afterthought, as though my craving for nicotine is reduced by the casualness of the encounter, as though I live on the street and make the purchases of street people in passing. The woman serving at the counter barely looks at me and I think how invisible I have become. She takes two cigarettes from an open box of thirty and retrieves the matches from a yellow packet behind her and in one movement slaps them down and takes up the exact change from the counter. There's no thank you or acknowledgement to close the transaction; it's as though it never happened.

I leave the shop and there's a woman standing outside, on the other side of the door. She looks familiar and expectant; for a moment I think I know her, and then I know I do not. She catches my eye and puts a hand out to touch my arm before she speaks. 'Do you have a light?'

I notice the cigarette perched lightly in the air between her two fingers. I fumble with the things in my hands, the change and the matches and the cigarettes, and then I hand her the matches, just bought. I don't light it for her, I just hand her the box.

'You shouldn't smoke at a petrol station,' I tell her, and then cringe at the teacher's voice in me that comes out always, no matter where or what else I am. Or am not. She laughs lightly and says, 'Of course. Let's go and stand over there on the grass away from the danger.' She makes me laugh awkwardly at my own caution, and makes me follow her.

On the grass she pulls out a full-but-one box of cigarettes from her jeans pocket and offers it to me. I show her the two cigarettes just bought but she tell me to save them for later. 'I'm afraid I'm still fully addicted,' she says. 'I've been trying to give up since I was eighteen.' She looks about my own age but prettier, although her face is beginning to show the deep marks of her life.

'I can't do without my two a day,' I tell her. 'At the end of it they're a kind of reward.'

She laughs again and tells me she knows what I mean. With steady fingers she lights both our cigarettes with a match from my box. 'I walk every day,' she tells me, 'but I even sometimes stop to smoke on my walk. How bad is that.' She says it as a statement, not a question, and I can think of nothing to say in return.

She tells me her name when we've both been puffing a while, with me caught in an uncomfortable silence. I nod and before I can tell her my own she says, 'You look like you're a walker too.'

'Every day. I'm a teacher at a school not far from here. Special ed. I need to walk off my job in the afternoons.'

'Teacher, hey? That must be a fascinating job. All those kids.' She smokes like she really means it, like it's a ventilator that makes her live. 'I almost became a teacher once. When I thought I was going to fail as a writer.'

'You're a writer?'

'Yes.'

'What sort?'

'Books, novels, fiction. And then anything else for money.' The way she says it is almost throwaway, as though the fact of her success makes it almost unimportant. But it also grants me permission to confess to what most people in my life don't know.

'I wanted to write once,' I say, bravely. 'Or I thought about it anyway.'

She turns her eyes upon me, deeply serious, and the way she speaks makes me think of myself, how I must look to my learners when I talk to them slowly, carefully, trying to maximise understanding in a situation of limitations. 'You shouldn't have stopped,' she says. 'I nearly did, hundreds of times.'

'What's your last name?' I ask her. 'Would I know your stuff?'

She tells me her name and I do a double take in spite of myself; I literally look at her twice.

She nods in response, sheepishly, as though I've discovered her by accident, as though her name does not matter as much as the encounter we're having. I wonder if it's her way of masking pride, or perhaps she's embarrassed. I know her books, and then I know why I thought I recognised her outside the shop. I've seen her picture before. I've watched her career with a secret twinge of envy, perhaps a certain sorrow for myself.

'I've read your books,' I say. 'Everyone knows you. I didn't know you lived around here.' Immediately she takes the attention off herself, places it squarely onto me. 'What you do is pretty amazing,' she says. I like to hear that, it's what everybody says when they hear that I'm a teacher, but I know it isn't true. What I think they're really saying is, how can you do such hard work for so little money, and at your age? They think I chose my work and that makes me some kind of martyr, that there's something different, special about me. What they don't know is that I don't have the chutzpah to choose anything, to do anything else. 'How did you get into it?' she asks.

'I lived in London for a bit. I did an education degree so I could get work easily there. I never got out of it. I carried on when I came back home.'

'Wow,' she says, and I think it's because she's lost for anything else to say. 'You must be a special type of person.' I don't know what that means either; or should I rather say again, I know it isn't true. I'm a lazy type of person, a self-defeating type of person. But then she surprises me. 'I also lived in London. Very early in my life when I started to get serious about what I wanted to do.'

I nod and stub out the end of my cigarette, but I don't answer because I don't want to go on with the conversation. I walk to get away from my work, even for a few evening hours. I don't want to talk about the pain, the loss, the fear, the extraordinary vulnerability of the children. I don't want to reduce their world to politeness for the sake of conversation.

Her cigarette is finished too, but she quickly lights another one with the matches, but this time there's no second offer for me. 'Don't go yet,' she says. 'Stay with me while I smoke some more.'

The evening settles into the soft orange glow that often comes after the rain. The streets are silver wet and the cars glisten as they pass. Men hurry homewards with bags on their backs, women shake their umbrellas before they close them and I watch the tiny drops spray about.

'So why did you stop writing?' she asks me. I don't want to talk about this either, my dream, my failure and defeat; and yet her eyes are bearing down on me, cool, clear, blue. Her face is lined, but timeless. The kind of face I wanted for myself as the years wore on.

'I never really started,' I said. 'I wrote a few short stories, a couple of poems when I was younger. It was just a dream I had, once.'

She nods as though she knows. 'A lot of people dream of writing,' she says, but I know she knows nothing. She's tasted the sweetness of success; after that, the hardship just becomes part of it, a right of passage. But what does that passage mean when there's nothing at the end of it, I want to ask her. I want to jab my finger into her shoulder and tell her meanly that she knows fuck all about life and what it's like to live in the world, but I know that this is just jealousy, simply a longing to be more than I am. It's not about her at all.

'Are you married?' she asks suddenly, and I nod.

'Children?'

'No.'

'Me neither,' she says, and looks away briefly, across the road. 'When my clock started ticking I really felt I had to make that choice. I was afraid of motherhood, that it would make me look at the world in a different way, that a child would smother the writer in me. Force me to forget how to really look at things, you know? My husband didn't care one way or the other, so it was a natural process for us not to do it. I'm glad, now, that I'm still free.' She seems so sure of herself, this woman who has her life sorted, who has reached professional success with her afternoons free to walk the suburbs and the moral decision of children all wrapped up so neatly. The thing that I hate, I think, is that I actually like her. I put one of the lose cigarettes to my lips, and she immediately strikes a match for me, from my box.

'Children suck the life out of you, from what I've seen,' she continues as I'm sucking at the cigarette, bringing it to life. 'People stop living, as though kids are an excuse to stop doing things, to stop learning, to stop taking responsibility for anything else. You become narrow, stupid, you develop tunnel vision. I don't want to be like that. And then the kids grow up and they resent you for what you've become in the process of giving everything in your life to them anyway.'

I say nothing, but she won't allow my silence. She's shared her cigarettes and in return she wants my conversation. 'And you?' she asks. 'Does your husband want kids?'

'No.'

'Do you?'

'Not really. You'd think I would have got to it before now, if I did. It's getting a bit late for me. And I work with children all day anyway.' I am, of course, lying. I want children, I want something small and soft and needy to fill the place of emptiness I see stretching on in me forever, but I cannot tell this woman that I am broken, that I work with broken children and I should have never married and I should have pursued the writing and I envy the days that she is free to walk and to write forever. I cannot tell her that my powerlessness makes me believe that it's possible my womb is broken too, that I am capable of producing a being that is broken and incomplete. I have seen too many children turn out not as anyone expected.

'Nah, if you really want them, if you really want anything, it's never too late,' she says. 'You can always make a plan.' She's glib, she makes me want to believe in something in her words but as my life touches hers so briefly outside this petrol station it's as though I'm touching one of her books. It's real, but only in the context of a story. It is not really life.

Out of politeness and a need to shift the attention away from myself, I ask her a question: 'Are you working on anything at the moment?'

She looks at me sideways, hesitates before she speaks. 'I don't usually talk about my work before it's down on the paper and written,' she says. 'It's a kind of superstition of mine, like once it's out before it's written it will lose its power. But you're different, somehow. Like you wouldn't judge it.' She pauses, waiting for a response, some encouragement, but I'm wary of anything that sounds like flattery. She goes on anyway. 'It's another novel. Fiction. It's about a guy who fakes his own death in order to live the life he really wants to. But as a character he remains on the periphery. The real action happens to the people around him, the ones who gather to mourn him.'

I smile at her, and nod. It's so simple, so straightforward; like something I could have dreamed up or imagined myself. I want to leave now, to continue my walk alone and I tell her so, but there's a feeling in me that there's something I've forgotten, or that I'm about to leave behind. 'Good luck with your kids,' she says. 'My mother always said that if you can help people and make enough to live on from it, you'll live a better life than most.'

When she says goodbye it's casual and friendly and reduces me to my place in her world, a passing stranger from whom she could cadge a match, share a smoke, the briefest time of day. There was nothing more in it for her, and she turns away from me, walks off down the road, and I wonder if I'll ever appear in any of her stories in any meagre form. Then I hear her voice again, calling at my back. 'Hey!' she says, and I turn around. 'I forgot to ask your name.'

I laugh, a real, genuine chuckle, and I hear it carried into the traffic along with my reply. 'Same as yours,' I call back, and she laughs too.

'Go well then,' she says. '*Hamba kahle*. Maybe I'll see you again one day on my walks.'

When she's gone I look down at my remaining cigarette, but she's taken my box of matches with her.

I walk until my heartbeat matches the rhythm of my feet. I walk until the traffic drone dies with the day and is replaced by the voices in my head, speaking to me of children, and longing, and work, and the relentless days ahead. I walk with the people on the road to know that I am real, to deliver myself to the world as I withdraw further from the life of people, and into the realm of the soul where those half-living and those half-dead collide on a painted island mid-way between. As I said, it's been done before, this meeting of the self on a lonely road. It's not an original idea, just like there's nothing about my own life that's novel or new.

Muthal Naidoo

The Bridge-Playing Rain Queens

Four refugees from the ARP&P (Association of Retired Persons and Pensioners) – they couldn't play bridge you see – put their grey heads together and decided to form their own bridge club. They would teach themselves the game. Etta, short for Martinetta, a former teacher, set up the course and was very strict. She made learning aids, gave homework and administered tests. Prudence, widow of a former diplomat, devoted herself to protocol and made sure that they all followed proper bridge etiquette – everything clockwise and to the right. Hilary, member of a mountaineering club, challenged the group to go higher and higher and while they struggled to master bidding, finessing and ruffing, Felicity kept their spirits up with amusing tales about Whiskey, her seventeen-year-old cat.

The first time the group met to play bridge the heavens opened up and flooded the whole city. A clever motor engineer, stalled by the deluge and watching the rising tide outside his window, had a brainwave – a car with oars or an outboard motor – and was destined to spend the rest of his life trying to design such a machine.

Felicity and Whiskey, looking out at the torrent, were glad that they had brought in the washing before the downpour. On the following Friday morning, when the group sat down to play, it came down in buckets again and every Friday after that. Umbrellas and raincoats became essential requirements for a bridge game. When Hilary went off on a hike and Felicity out of town to a grandchild's twenty-first birthday party, they stopped playing for a couple of weeks and the weather was fine.

On the Friday morning that they resumed their sessions, it began to pour again and they were caught without raincoats and umbrellas. Etta, an avid reader of science fiction, saw in it a paranormal phenomenon. The following Friday, after the women had trooped through Whiskey's garden carrying raincoats and umbrellas as had been their wont before the break, and had settled around the card table, Etta made a dramatic announcement, 'I have been contacted by aliens.' Whiskey jumped off the sofa, ran into the bedroom and disappeared under the bed.

'You can't be serious.' Prudence was sceptical.

But Felicity was quite amazed. 'Did you see Whiskey's reaction? I've never seen him scurry off like that before. He thinks he's only twelve.'

A mystical glow filled cat-lover Hilary's eyes. 'The only other time I have seen such a reaction was when our mountaineering club visited Kathmandu. The Dalai Lama's cat, which he had left behind, streaks through the streets at odd times. Tibetans see him as a symbol of their ultimate liberation.'

Not being fond of cats, Etta interrupted with a portentous announcement, 'I was given a message.' Her solemn look silenced the others. 'My phone rang!' This was extraordinary indeed. 'When I answered, a weird voice said, *This is Vodac*. He gabbled on in a pseudo-American accent and I couldn't make out what he was saying....'

'Were you wearing your hearing aids?' Prudence was finding this conversation quite ludicrous.

'I don't need them when I'm on the phone. In any event, it

didn't matter that I couldn't make out the words, I understood instinctively.'

'Oh really? What did you understand?' Prudence would have guffawed but crude noises were foreign to her.

'Just look out of the window. Do you see?' They didn't. 'It's clear. Not a cloud in the sky, not a drop of rain. It is a beautiful sunshine and braaivleis day. That's how it always is before we begin to play.' Etta paused significantly. 'The minute we start, it comes pouring down.'

'You don't really believe that!' Prudence couldn't hide the smile.

Felicity was nodding thoughtfully. 'It does rain every time we play, doesn't it?'

'The Aztecs had ways of communing with the gods.' Hilary turned to Etta, 'Are you sure you were contacted by aliens? Not Aztec spirit guides?'

Prudence was losing patience. 'Oh please. This is nonsense and you know it.'

Etta smiled back knowingly. 'Let's play and you'll see.'

Felicity picked up the cards and shuffled. As she dealt, the light began to change. As soon as she called one club, day disappeared under an overcast sky. When the bidding was over and Pru had contracted for game, thunder and lightning broke free and the clatter of raindrops on the roof drowned out all attempts at conversation except, of course, for Etta's guffawed, 'What did I tell you?'

Pru reluctantly raised her voice: 'But what have aliens to do with the rain?'

'They have given us the power to end the drought.'

Prudence couldn't believe her ears. 'With bridge!'

But Etta, inspired, jumped up with evangelistic fervour. 'We will drive down to Bloemfontein and help the mielie boers whose crops are failing.'

Hilary, who loved challenges, cheered while Pru, who was finding it difficult to control her disdain, inquired in mocking tones, 'What do you propose? That we set up a card table in the middle of a maize field?'

'Exactly!'

Hilary nodded. 'What have we got to lose?'

'What will I do with Whiskey?'

'Put him in cat care.'

Despite Pru's protests, the next thing she knew they were in the middle of the mielielands sweltering in a tent under a clear blue sky. Etta had insisted on the tent to protect them from the rain. Within minutes of setting up their table, a few clouds sailed in over the horizon. As soon as Pru started to deal, the sky became overcast. As she opened the bidding, she heard the first big drops splattering among the dry cobs. When she made the game call of 3 No Trumps, the heavens opened up.

Pru was forced to concede.

And the four women understood and accepted! They had been called to serve their country, to avert a national crisis.

Once the nation understood, their lives changed altogether and they were flying from province to province bringing succour to farmers everywhere.

People hailed them as saviours.

Except, of course, at Cycadia. Pulamvula, the Official Rain Queen (ORQ), was in a state of despair. It had not rained since the old queen had died, since she had become ORQ. People looked at her askance. They were beginning to doubt her powers and were losing faith in the age-old tradition. To make matters worse, these bridge players had come out of nowhere and broken the drought. Every time she switched on the TV in her hut and saw the weatherman showing where the bridge players would be, she turned into a raging fury, dancing, stamping and ululating, bringing down the most violent electric storms but not a drop of rain. Nevertheless, *She* was the Queen, anointed by God! Not the surrogate of alien creatures from another planet! She would not allow the pretenders to usurp her throne! She consulted the *inkosi,* threw the bones and saw that she had to depose the upstarts if she was ever to get her powers back. So she went on TV news and during the weather forecasts challenged the bridge group to a rainmaking contest at Cycadia.

They were stunned, but felt obliged to accept.

On the appointed day, the cycad-enclosed arena was crowded with spectators and crews from TV networks sent to broadcast the event live across the country. After establishing the setting, cameras focused on the *Sangoma* flanked by her drummers, then panned to the opposite side where the bridge players, in their tent, sat upright at their card table, their packs shuffled and ready. Each side had one hour to bring down the rain. When the signal was given, Queen Pulamvula, who had won the toss, threw a contemptuous look at the bridge group and began to dance. Her drummers struggled to keep up with her pace and vigour as she blew her whistle, flailed her *chobo,* leaped, shouted and ululated. Lightning streaked the sky, struck an empty hut nearby and set it alight. Thunder crashed like an invading army. But no rain. Not one drop. At the end of her hour, Pulamvula sank to the ground with a terrible groan.

The cameras then zoomed in on the bridge players. Hilary dealt and they took up their cards. They were very nervous and the bidding began tentatively. But they soon got into their stride and when Pru called a small slam, nimbus clouds threw a pall over the sky. As Hilary led the first card and Felicity put her dummy hand on the table, large drops began a loud tattoo on the ground. Then sheets of rain slanted over the earth. People raced off in all directions and TV crews disappeared into vans. Only Queen Pulamvula, collapsed in despair at the centre of the arena, lay there calling on the lightning to strike her dead. A drenched, writhing bundle, she did not see the umbrella and raincoat brigade moving towards her. It was only when she felt Felicity's hand on her shoulder that she saw the bridge players kneeling beside her. Felicity spoke quietly to her and after some minutes, the queen stood up slowly in all her dignity, and returned to her hut.

The next year when it was time for the rainy season, Queen Pulamvula danced and it rained and rained and rained. She broke the drought and was restored to her rightful place as the country's ORQ.

Now people come from all over the world to see her perform her miracle.

If you ever go to Cycadia to catch a glimpse of the queen during the rainy season, leave the beaten track and you will find, hidden among the cycads, a little tent in which four women contentedly play bridge while Pulamvula dances.

Mary Watson Seoighe

The Lilitree

Quinton planted the Lilitree in the back garden. It wasn't much of a garden, muddy with patchy flowers and weeds growing haphazardly, scrawny tomato plants dwarfed by a monster crop of broad beans. Lilitrees are, of course, illegal and very rare. No one knows where they're from, but in the old days you'd find them mostly in the sandy areas, in the notorious Cape Flats. And also near water; they always move towards water. But you don't find them so much these days, not for a long time. Just now and then you hear of one. But Quinton had connections.

He bought the seed at twilight in a little alley off Main Road. He went right at the minibus taxi rank, past the Virgin Active gym where people were eerily framed in the lit windows, jogging up and down. He wove his way through the tattooed men out looking for trouble, until he came to the crossroads where Adultworld and the post office meet. The dealer sheltered in the doorway of an old abandoned Victorian building, smoking a pipe. Quinton could not see the face of his supplier, which was hidden in the folds of the long cape. Rough hands dropped the seed into a brown paper bag, knotted it with string and furtively took the wad of notes.

Quinton planted the Lilitree beneath the exposed roots of the cabbage tree before Marlene could stop him. When she found out that they were to grow a little girl in the muddy backyard, she was livid.

'How are we supposed to feed her? We just don't have the money, Quinton. Use your head for once in your life.' She headed to the yard, her sinking heels leaving a fine track in the mud. Marlene, down on her knees, was about to unearth the seed when Quinton's voice came from behind her: 'You can't do that, it's – it's abortion.' Marlene, who was still grappling with the residual effects of her early years as a Catholic, wouldn't speak to him for days.

But nothing happened. Every day Quinton checked the spot where he had planted the Lilitree, but the caked brown soil yielded nothing. Marlene wore an insufferably smug tight-lipped smile. She whistled primly while she washed and ironed the huge bags of other people's clothes that made her hands so reddish raw. When they saw the dreaded Kikuyu grass springing up like uninvited guests, Quinton began to feel he had been taken for a ride. And the seed hadn't come cheap – he had used a month of Friday night drink money to pay for it.

'Just think how many more bags of dirty clothes we could wash, if she did it for us. And we'd never need get up to change the TV channel ever again,' Quinton sighed as he poked Marlene up to change the TV channel. They didn't have a remote control for their old box.

That weekend, Marlene was about to uproot the grass before it could spread and cover their nice muddy yard, when she noticed something different. A patch of grass had grown into thin green fingers, spread out on top of the soil and gently pressing down as if about to hoist out of the mud. She screamed.

The next day, a little head appeared, like a cabbage sprung up overnight. Every day their Lilitree grew and grew: first firm green stalk-like arms, then a barky brownish green trunk, then the long muddy tendrils that coiled and snaked down her back, until by the end of the month, there was a little girl growing in the garden.

'When can we pick her?' asked Marlene, who was tired of doing the dishes. Quinton never helped with the housework, never mind their laundry service. He liked to think of himself as the public relations department, answering the phone and greeting the customers, especially the nice ladies. Marlene ached with the strain on her back; she most hated bending over the bath to wash the delicates.

'We can't pick her – she has to walk out of the pod. The instructions say that she will come knocking at the door.'

Now it was Marlene who was the more eager to have their Lilitree ready for harvest. She covered her feet (a bit like exposed roots) with compost, including nice wriggling maggots that made the Lilitree shudder. Marlene, despite the rain, watered the tree every day until the little girl cried from the relentless cold spray.

'Aw, shut it,' yawned Marlene, 'otherwise we will eat you.'

The Lilitree cried louder in her little cat-like voice. The August rain lashed down and she caught a cold and sniffed miserably. (Lilitrees can only be planted in early July, otherwise they just turn into cabbages.)

'A bit of a wet blanket,' Marlene nodded to Quinton, 'I should give her something to cry about.'

Throughout September Marlene continued to nurture their little tree as it grew steadily. By November Quinton was bored with it all. But still the Lilitree did not step out of her pod. The mangy stray cats came and hissed at the tree and she hissed back.

Marlene waited impatiently. They thought up names for her; they tried to coax her into the house by waving nice sweeties and marshmallows at the window. In late spring, the Lilitree started to grow little green breasts. Marlene found it quite indecent and covered them with a kitchen cloth.

Finally, during a sweltering week in late December, there was a knock at the kitchen window, a small tentative tap-tap. Marlene and Quinton were watching TV and almost didn't hear it. 'Hello mommy,' said Quinton kissing Marlene, 'I think that's our little girl!'

But the Lilitree was not a little girl. There, standing at the kitchen door was a fully grown woman. Green with barky skin, she had fashioned a shift made of rubble bags and swung the red checked dish towel around her waist. Quinton had never seen a more beautiful woman.

'You idiot!' Marlene shouted at Quinton. 'You got the wrong seed.'

'It's your fault,' Quinton shouted back, 'if you hadn't watered her so much and rubbed all that compost on her feet ...'.

But he remembered guiltily how the seed dealer had been standing too close to Adultworld. Maybe this was a different kind of Lilitree?

'We can look it up on the Internet,' he pacified Marlene.

'Please can I have some water?' rasped the Lilitree, leaning against the doorframe.

'Look at the poor girl,' Quinton fussed. 'Marlene, get her some tea!'

Quinton was enchanted by the fragile creature that took on their household tasks with an impassive vigour. Not only did she do all the housework, but she also washed an inordinate number of dirty clothes. Marlene was pleased. Soon they could afford a new TV, with remote control.

But the Lilitree couldn't settle. She preferred bedding down in the mud beneath the cabbage tree. She shunned the tasty sausages that Marlene made and rummaged through the compost heap for her supper. She drank greedily the water that gushed straight from the outside tap into her mouth. She loved the hosepipe. She tracked mud into the house, her dirty toes against the scrubbed tiles. And best, she worked like a demon. But even as hundreds of great big white laundry bags were effortlessly dispatched, the Lilitree was weighted down as if by an invisible burden. There was a forlornness about her that stirred Quinton's curiosity. When Marlene tried to lock her inside during the heavy rains, the Lilitree stared out at the garden and yearned for the smells, the soft and varied textures of the scraggly plants that grew there, the feel of the rain against her skin. She didn't seem interested in much else. One night, as she brought them hot chocolate during their favourite shows, they discovered that she liked reality TV. She watched with them and once she even laughed out loud, like the sound of wind rustling leaves. But after a few nights of intent viewing, she lost interest. Halfway through *The Peepshow*, she wandered out and Quinton found she had climbed high up the cabbage tree, with its branches wrapped around her.

Quinton tried to console her with magazines and chocolates. First she grabbed them greedily, ripping through the celebrity pictures while sucking the soft caramel out of the chocolates. Not long after, magazines lay unopened; chocolates were trodden into the mud. He bought her a pretty yellow dress, which brought out the colour of her skin and she danced around in it, delighted. Marlene found it two days later, in the vegetable patch, like a dirty pumpkin. Quinton gave her flowers, but the Lilitree shrieked when she saw her cut sisters and laid them tenderly in her muddy bed. Quinton crept beneath the cabbage tree where she lay, and listened to her unhappy woody breathing.

Marlene observed silently. She watched those long elegant fingers wringing sheets, ironing and folding the endless stacks of shirts and trousers. She watched the Lilitree bending over the tub to wash the delicates, her body gently swaying.

Marlene thought of taking a nice Sunday afternoon walk in the forest with the Lilitree. Because they were one happy family. They veiled her greenish skin with a coat and shawls and tied back her thick tendrils with scarves. They entered the forest with the tightly wrapped woman and immediately, when she smelt the damp wood and leaves, she bolted, pulling at the jacket and scarves that bound her. She ran off the path and was easily camouflaged by the trees. Quinton sprinted after her and they raced between the pines. He puffed behind her but she remained out of reach. She heard the low guttural tones first, but even so she was unprepared: turning a bend, she saw a great gush of water from beyond what was visible – right up to the clouds – and was entranced at the sight. Never had she seen such an enormous tap. Unable to resist, she paused for a second and drank from the spray of the waterfall. Hearing footsteps, she turned and ran, but Quinton had gained on her, and with a flying leap, rugby tackled her to the ground. They rolled in the moss and stones. He loved her then; no one had ever been lovelier. He couldn't let her go, he told her beneath the insistent chatter of the waterfall. She begged and pleaded to stay in the forest with the other trees and the giant tap. But Quinton couldn't. So, in his arms, he carried her back to the car and Marlene drove them home. Heading back to the disquieted suburbs, they all felt let down.

The Lilitree could not forget the forest. The little muddy yard was suddenly too small because she could hear a distant whisper of trees from beyond those high cracked walls; she heard the call of the sea she had never seen. She thought only of the water gushing from the mountain spring and lost her taste for the outside tap.

Marlene also dreamed of the forest. She dreamed of the Lilitree being eaten by porcupines, of the manky smell of rotting wood, of lightning severing limbs with branched out fingers and a slow death by ants. In her dreams she tried to help, she was always coming with a basket of sweets and a bottle of milk and a bottle of gin. But she never got there.

Without water, the Lilitree's skin took on a greyish tinge and her fingers faded to yellow. Her limber gait slowed down and her movements worked to an arthritic grind. Quinton hovered, eager to do anything she wanted, but for the one thing that the Lilitree asked of him.

'You wouldn't be safe there,' he pleaded with her. Then, more assertively, 'I am responsible for you.'

She stopped eating decaying vegetables from the compost heap. She cowered when Quinton sprayed her with the hosepipe.

'Let me go back,' she asked again. But Quinton could not.

The Lilitree wilted. Her face lined with faint concentric rings that deepened as if scored into her skin. On the day that she could no longer lift the heavy laundry bags, she raised herself from the delicates and found that she hurt in a way that she had never hurt before. She went to lay herself beneath the cabbage tree, her trunk held within its roots. There she stayed, and her skin turned a silvery brown, and the leaves swished above her.

They never talked about her after that. Later, they forgot that, for almost a year, they had known and even loved a tree woman. When their children played in the garden, beneath the two cabbage trees, they knew only a vague story about how Quinton had carried the silver bough from the forest, and how, soon after, the second tree had sprouted from its trunk.

WILLEMIEN DE VILLIERS

Coming in to Land

'In the unlikely event of decompression ...' a voice starts, and I turn my gaze towards the window. Lately, I don't like the look of oxygen masks. Just before take-off I have a brief vision of an explosion, obliterating the entire airport building. And then we lift up, and away from my imagined danger. Now, my eyes catch a glimpse of sparkle below, a car overtaking a slow truck. Another shimmer approaches from the opposite direction: the two vehicles narrowly miss. Even if a head-on collision occurred, I would remain unaffected.

Instead, I look at a faded blue serpentine river below. Next to it, a cluster of circular sewerage tanks offers a strange patterned beauty.

The familiar Cape Town landscape recedes and is gradually replaced by a two-dimensional rust-coloured map, contoured by several pale, flat-topped ridges. The plane noses through a dense cloud; small puffs drift free to float above their shadows, which form dark splatters on the landscape below. Human imprint is visible everywhere, in the precise geometry of agriculture, the ploughed fields turned into pattern.

We fly over the flooded areas surrounding Arniston and

Bredasdorp, where I met my father for the last time. He made the trip from Johannesburg, to introduce me to his place of birth. We walked and talked; found an old abandoned *bakoond* in the veld and agreed that the yeasty smell of freshly baked bread still lingered in the air. My father was a shy but violent man. Although I had longed to take his hand as we walked, I didn't, because I knew he would fluster and pull at the collar of his shirt and lengthen his stride, so that my hand would slip free of his.

Breakfast is being served. I order two whiskies, and register a flicker of interest from the man sitting next to me. The top of the first miniature bottle twists open with a satisfying snap of the seal. I empty it over the ice cubes in the plastic cup on the tray.

'We are approaching Kimberley now, on the right,' the captain's voice announces, and I notice a large X-shape, close to the familiar landmark Big Hole. I imagine God's fist punching, as I lift the cup to my lips in a silent toast to my father.

I try to decipher the landscape below. Cemeteries appear as enormous tablets, with the scattered headstones forming lines of coded text. Soon my father's stone, placed next to my mother's, will form part of this Morse code from the departed.

Last night I lay awake for a long time, watching grey flakes of ash sifting through the dense canopy of flowering gum trees outside my bedroom window. It formed a veil covering the burnt haunches of the mountain. Time – primordial, patient beast – kept me company. Along with first light, the sound of drums and singing appeared. Just before finally drifting into a deep sleep, I thought how strange it was that I could sense how this dawn song would end. The beginning of a song always carries a hint of the final note.

When I woke up, I touched the wooden box on my bedside table. Inside were letters I had spent the previous day reading, unopened letters my father had written to my mother.

My father no longer has time on his side.

What would the man next to me say if I should decide to tell him that my mother had died, not knowing that she was loved? I unscrew the lid of the second bottle, glancing at the title of the book he is reading, *Life among the Serial Killers*.

On that last day I spent with my father I also visited my mother's old friend, and doctor, who still lived in Bredasdorp. Dr Hilliard was, at age eighty-nine, still a handsome woman, although people warned me that her mind was gone. Platinum hair, worn very short, high cheekbones, and bright blue eyes. 'You look like your father,' she said, handing me the wooden box of sealed letters, along with a thick medical file. 'I never wanted him,' she said, 'but your mother was a fool.' Several of my mother's mammogram X-rays tumbled from the file to the floor.

'She was always going on about being locked inside a room,' the doctor continued, 'waiting for the flames to devour her.' She wagged a finger at me, and gave a throaty laugh. 'But that room had a door, and the door had a key. And she was the keeper of the key. Don't ever forget that,' she said, fixing her eyes on mine.

I bent down to pick up the dropped X-rays. A nebulous map of maternal tissue was visible against the glossy black background, contoured by the outline of my mother's breasts.

After another mouthful of whisky, I close my eyes to call my dream lover to me. We know each other well, although we have never met. I am inside one of the many rooms of his house. These rooms have no doors. Everywhere is openness, and light. He is a lovely, large man. He walks to me, and holds me. While talking, the palms of his hands keep contact with my bare skin; moving slowly over my upper back, dipping into my waist, caressing my soft, round hips. Every now and then, he stops talking, and kisses me. Slow kisses that feed a hunger I was unaware of. 'In this world,' he whispers, 'it is important to show your pain.' He guides my hands to push up his shirt, revealing a multitude of tracings, faint tribal scars.

Deep sadness forces me to open my eyes. I notice another river below. This one forms a convoluted, jagged line, and seems to knit the skull of the earth together.

The first mine dumps appear.

Not long now.

Amanda Gersh

Home Helper

The Salute

Mike Pringle walks with his hands on his hips, watching as men push wheelbarrows around the side of the house. 'Over here, boys,' he says, pointing to the back of the garden, where other men push machines and smear cement. He is building a tennis-court.

'Lumka, bhuti! Carefully, hey,' Mike says when one of the men nearly tips cement onto the lawn. But Mike says it nicely, and he even jokes with them in Xhosa when they take their lunchbreak. He even sits and drinks coffee with them, and even from a tin mug like theirs. He is so nice, and to everyone. It doesn't matter who he is talking to, he is always a very nice man, Julie thinks, watching him. And she would know. Isn't he nice enough to build her this tennis-court?

I'm so lucky! Julie thinks, as the men pick up their shovels and get back to work.

All afternoon she watches them and all afternoon she thinks how lucky she is to have a father like Mike Pringle. How did he even know she wanted a tennis-court? She didn't even have to ask, she just pictured it in her mind and next thing you know, there are garden boys and builders everywhere, sharing a laugh with her dad while she watches.

A tennis-court. A tennis-court for tennis and also for fairies to play on.

The court takes shape underneath the shade of Table Mountain. Julie listens to the turtle-doves making their lazy afternoon sounds. When the shadows stretch, Mike Pringle hunts for his car keys. It's time for Julie to go home.

The Promise

'I promise to do my best. To love God and to serve my country. To help others. And to keep the Brownie Law.' Julie chants her Promise and when she is finished she is asked to hold hands with her neighbours and start the group friendship squeeze. She is a Brownie now.

This moment has been top of Julie's list for three months. She has wanted the brown uniform – brown hat, brown skirt, brown shirt, yellow necktie – ever since Tracy-Ann Pringle moved from Port Elizabeth and became her best friend. Tracy-Ann has a full sleeve of badges with little pictures on them – house, fire, ball, rope, music note.

Julie wants the badges because they are beautiful and she wants them because she wants to be the same as Tracy-Ann. Tracy-Ann has a beautiful and busy family and they live in an airy Constantia house with mint-coloured carpets and walls that look like bedspreads, covered with patterns made of fabric. Their lawn arrived in a special truck. Julie saw it get rolled on.

Mrs Pringle has a blond swinging bob that leaves a perfume taste after she hugs you. She is tremendously thin and is a judge in the Bokomo Baking competition, going to all the schools and tasting scones from all the individual ovens. She did not seem to notice that Julie's scones were flat. 'Delicious,' she said to Julie, and winked.

Mr Pringle makes Julie shy because he is too handsome. He has gold cat eyes and exceptionally red lips. He has brown muscular arms, pink shirts with crocodiles on the pockets, legs without hair on them. He says *'call me Mike.'*

Mr Pringle *call me Mike* owns lots of companies – paper factories, chains of Stirrups steak houses – but he does lots of other things too like driving the Standard Five hockey team to Jonkershoek and directing the flower arranging at Julie and Tracy-Ann's school for special occasions. Julie has seen him poke pincushion proteas into green sponge Oasis, teaching the mums and the teachers, talking about texture and colour and seeds because he is on the board of Kirstenbosch and he knows all about these things, he is even writing a book and doing the pictures himself. He is, as Julie's teacher once said, a worthy man, though Julie does not quite understand the meaning of worthy, but it sounds good, strong; it sounds worthy.

The Handshake

'Lend a hand.' Julie chants the motto and steps back from the circle with the other Brownies, holding three fingers to her Brownie hat in the special Brownie way.

When she demonstrates this at home and explains how the Brownies' international handshake is with the left hand, her father frowns and says it's very strange this left-handed business. Julie says no it's not and her father argues, saying since the time of Jesus and the time of Allah nobody in the world shakes with the left hand because the left hand is for wiping, the left hand is just plain wrong, left is sinister, it's even called *sinistra* in Italy. Julie says rubbish but her father says this is a universal truth, she must ask the Jewish girls, ask the Muslim girls at her school if she doesn't believe it, ask any of the African girls even, you don't see them in Brownie uniforms now, do you? But Julie knows her father is just in a bad mood because he didn't sell the show house today and anyway there is an Indian girl at Brownies who is even a leader.

Julie's mom tells her father to shh and says who cares about God. Her father says it's not God we're talking about, it's wiping, and her mother says why are we making lavatorial conversation? She asks Julie about the lady who runs the Brownie troop and Julie describes her grey curls and blue uniform, her British accent and the skin wobble under her chin. Sounds like a bit of a missionary scene if you ask me, her dad says, lighting a cigarette, but Julie defends Brown Owl and her deputy, Tawny Owl, because they welcomed her to Brownies and gave her a choice of being a tortoise or a dassie, Brown Owl pronouncing tortoises tor-*toyce*-es. Julie wanted to be a bush baby like Tracy-Ann, she knew their song by heart before she joined – *We're bush babies keen and bright, serving others day and night* – but the bush babies are already six and all full up, so Julie is a tortoise. *Here we are the tortoise six, helping others in a fix.* 'That's a lovely song darling,' her mother says, yawning. 'What fun!'

But Brownies is not fun. The tortoise group project is making beaded tea cosies with periwinkle shells on the ends for an old people's home. This is slow and boring. The whole tortoise group is slow and boring and the girls fight over beads and criticise each other's cosies. Worse, Julie hardly even sees Tracy-Ann because, apart from being a bush baby and the leader of bush babies, Tracy-Ann is very important in the whole of their Brownie unit. She has jobs that take her out of the hall, and spends time talking one-to-one with Tawny Owl next to the juice trays, writing things on charts.

Julie's first day is not good. After an hour spent with the tortoises on the cosies, she is supposed to select an activity and work towards earning her first Brownie badge, but she can't focus. She wanders through the hall watching Brownies practise their skipping, watching them paint and plan projects of one kind or another. She watches a group making reef-knots. She goes over. She tries to make a knot. She makes half a knot but it's not very good because her mind has already wandered, over to the music group, to the girl holding xylophones and recorders. A recorder! Julie lasts almost the whole morning with the recorder. She learns how to play *d* and *b* and *a g*. The girl in charge is called Izaan Strauss. She has freckles on her eyelids and is very good at recorder, she can even play 'Sho-Sholoza.' Izaan Strauss plays 'Sho-Sholoza' over and over again. Julie tries 'Sho-Sholoza' but she can't get past the first three notes. She sniffs her recorder. It smells terrible! She wanders away.

In spite of the promising chant and uniform, Saturday mornings are a disappointment for Julie. They come and go, each as long and shapeless as the next. Julie wanders because she is bored and she wanders because she has always wandered, wherever she is. She has noticed that most girls her age do not wander. Most know what they are doing. They like where they are. This goes for the Brownies as well as the girls in her class. When the school photographer poses them, they never move, but Julie is always slightly blurred.

The Law

Brown Owl is very strict about badges. She is not like other Brown Owls in other units, that's what Tracy-Ann says. In other units, it's easy to get badges. You can get them fast, and before you know it, your sleeve is full. But the Brown Owl of Fernwood pack is tough. You have to take your time. You have to do much more to earn a badge. You have to prove yourself to be worthy.

Julie doesn't like this information. She is disappointed in Brown Owl's high standards and she doesn't like the long lists in her Brownie badge book:

Nature Lover Badge:
Research the Six animals in the Brownie library. Describe their habitats, diets, reproduction habits, and record your findings in a colourful and imaginative way.

> *Think of five ways we can conserve water. Try them and share your methods with your six by giving a memorised talk.*
>
> *Make two nature crafts from seeds, sticks, leaves, or other natural materials that you gather on your nature walks. Suggestions: a twig picture frame, a stick and seashell wind chime, a pine cone and peanut butter bird feeder, or seed pod Christmas decorations.*
>
> *Select a small one foot squared plot of grass on your lawn. Each morning and evening for two weeks, spend twenty minutes examining what insects or other small animals travel across your plot. Record their movements in a chart, referencing appearance, locomotion speed, activities. (Is the ant carrying a crumb? Did the aphid pause to chew on a blade of grass?)*
>
> *Find a local bird guide. In pencil, trace the pictures of five birds to be found in Southern Africa, taking care to label their defining features appropriately.*

Julie still likes and wants the badges themselves. But she cannot choose a list and get through it. Nature Lover is not even the worst. To get the Sick Nurse badge, for instance, you must show how to use your scarf as an arm sling. You must demonstrate the Heimlich manoeuvre on another Brownie, and learn how to take someone's pulse. That is just the beginning of Sick Nurse. To get the badge with the lovely compass shape there is also a lot to tick off. Julie reads about north and south and west and east. She reads about measuring distances and reading maps, about locating landmarks and giving directions. She thinks she could maybe learn to take a pulse and then draw one map. But that is not enough for a badge and anyway you can't mix it up. You have to follow what Brown Owl says in the book, all the way to the end.

> *Calculate the distance between your home and the following: Bloubergstrand, Cape Point, Stellenbosch, Lion's Head...*

Julie stops reading when the lists get too long. Her eyes wander off – they just can't stay on – the page.

Powwow

Though Julie dislikes Brownies, the powwow at the end of each meeting makes up for the meeting itself. She loves Brown Owl and Tawny Owl standing in front of the papier-maché toadstool with the girls around them in a circle. She loves the serious way of the words from Brown Owl's mouth; praise, scolding, Julie is less concerned with what the Owl is saying and more concerned with how she says it, with an importance that Julie herself feels as she stands next to the others, everyone in their brown uniform, everything the same every time.

Sometimes Julie says 'powwow' to herself, out loud. The words give her a little puff, a little powwow.

The circle is fun. But Julie enjoys Brownies most of all when it is over, when Tracy-Ann's father fetches them in the shiny microbus – the microbus full of the small watchful Pringle girls who have spindly brown legs, gold hair and red plump lips just like Tracy-Ann and her dad – the microbus bound for the minty Pringle rooms, for the blue bean-shaped pool, the lawn and tennis court, the homemade afternoon cakes and watercolour sets for everyone, the doll house. Doll's house! This is Julie's best. A doll's house built by Mr Pringle with tiny knives and forks bought from overseas. Everyone plays with the Pringle doll's house, even the Pringle mom and dad and when Julie sees Mr – sees *Mike* – Pringle set the miniature table with his slender beautiful fingers, she hates Tracy-Ann for looking so calm.

As for her own father, Julie has hoped he might learn a thing or two from Mike, but this has not happened. In fact, neither of her parents seems to understand the value of a Pringle life. If anything, they disapprove of the Pringle family. Julie cannot understand her mother, the flickering pale frowns from the bedroom window when Mike pulls up in the driveway to pick Julie up or drop her off. Julie tells her parents that Mr Pringle and Mrs Pringle, that Mike and Charlene are both extremely worthy people, they even have a foster son at home making bird houses in the garage with Mike's tools, but her mother says nothing, she just rolls her pearl necklace between her fingers and her father stabs his cigarette end into the air and says there is something *sinistra* going on when a man that pretty knows what to do with a pincushion protea, if you catch my drift.

First-Year Star

'For charity?' Julie's father frowns at the HeavenCent-A-Day piggy bank she has placed on the dinner table. 'What kind of charity?'

Julie gets defensive. What does he mean, what kind? The poor kind, obviously.

'You mean the church kind.' Julie's father looks at the cross on the pig's back, next to the slot. 'That's not the poor kind if you ask me.'

But Julie fights back. So what if the church is organising the collection? In the end the money is going to go to the poor children of the townships who live in shacks and have nothing, this is what Brown Owl said. Dad says believe it when I see it but Julie doesn't even bother to argue because it doesn't matter what anyone believes or even where that money goes, what matters is getting that piggy bank filled up. Julie needs to get a badge, the Home Helper badge, and if she doesn't collect one hundred one-cent pieces for the poor children of Africa, then she's going to have some big problems on her hands, like getting dropped from Brownies, which means Tracy-Ann will find a new best friend, someone with badges coming out of her ears, someone with a name like Izaan Strauss, leader of the duiker six, who has finished all her paths, Footpath, Road, and Highway, and who will replace Julie on those after-Brownies visits to the Pringle house! No. Julie defends the piggy bank and the poor children for all they are worth and they are worth a lot. How nice to think of other people, her mother says, with a tired smile, and Julie agrees, thinking of others, thinking of the Pringle family.

'I'm getting Water Baby,' Tracy-Ann had announced to Julie as they lay on Tracy-Ann's lawn the previous Saturday. 'I learned mouth to mouth on a dummy. By the time we go to camp, I'll be halfway down my second sleeve!'

Tracy-Ann smiles and Julie smiles back. Camp! Second sleeve! These are powerful words. Julie is very excited about the upcoming Brownie Pack Away camp in Buinskloof. In only three weekends she'll be going away from home. She'll be without her parents for the first time. And there will be no tea cosies, no boring Saturday in the cold Brownie hall. There will be tents. They will be outside. And Brown Owl has promised an activity that perks Julie up: each six will put on a special play for the others, performing in front of the campfire!

Julie can't wait for the play. It sounds almost as thrilling as the camp badge ceremony, the court of awards that will be held in Buinskloof. By now, she has seen Brown Owl award many badges during the last powpow of each month when there is a court of awards. Julie has seen Brown Owl shake numerous girls' left hands while presenting the badge with her right hand. She has watched Tawny show the proud Brownie where the patch must be sewn on the sleeve. Tawny looks closely at the sleeve, at the other badges there, and finds the exact right spot for the new award. In such exhilarating gold-thread-neat-square-left-handshake moments, Julie claps hardest of all the girls. In these moments, she forgets the lists and sees only the badges themselves. Brownies is so exciting! She vows to concentrate, to stop wandering from activity to activity, to stop doing just one bit of a list before switching to another list. She vows to work hard and get those squares for her own sleeve. *Next week*, Julie thinks, every week.

But lying next to Tracy-Ann this week on the Pringle lawn, Julie gets a shock: she has been a Brownie for ten months! Her First-Year Star is only two months away, meaning she will soon have a badge just for being a Brownie, just for showing up. A badge for nothing.

But what happens when Brown Owl shakes her hand but Tawny sees her empty sleeve? What happens then?

'I'm getting Home Helper,' Julie lies to Tracy-Ann. She feels instantly bad for the lie but good about the decision. Saying it will make it happen.

Home Helper will be easiest, because you get to do it at home, away from the hall and its mix of choices. With that one you just take your book home with you and tick off a list of tasks you must do – making the beds in the house, washing dishes and clothes, cooking a meal, collecting old clothes and money for the poor. Then your parents sign the list and the badge is yours. 'I nearly got it last week,' Julie adds, 'but I'll get it at the camp ceremony.'

Saying it makes it real, gives her a quick happy jolt. She sees a Buinskloof mountain river, a sunset powwow circle. The solemn brown faces of mountains make the ceremony more sacred. Julie steps forward to receive her badge. Tracy-Ann claps hardest of all the girls. They are two best friends with badges.

Except that camp is not even a month away, and Julie has done nothing on the Home Helper list. She panics and plots. She regrets being so quick. She plucks out tufts of grass. It is very soft, this Pringle lawn. The blades are bright and tiny, the kind meant for golf. She puts them in her mouth.

'Home Helper. That's good,' Tracy-Ann says, but her look is far away, her eyes gleam with second-sleeve shapes. Boat. Mountain. Telescope.

Julie chews the lawn, watching Tracy-Ann. Tracy seems to have no idea how little Julie has done at Brownies, and this must mean that she is already too far from Julie, she is on a Highway and speeding into the distance. In the beginning, she used to remind and encourage Julie and even sweetly lecture her, but lately she seems to have forgotten that Julie is even a Brownie at all, and who could blame her? Julie thinks, chewing hard.

If I go mad this month, if I make all the beds and do all the dishes and collect all the coins, I can get that badge in three weeks in

Buinskloof, and if I get that badge in three weeks in Buinskloof then by the time I get my First-Year Star in two months, by the time the Tawny holds up that badge, points at my sleeve, and Brown Owl says well done Julie of the tor-toyce-es, there will be something on that sleeve and I will not get kicked out.

The Sign

'I don't think I remember how to do hospital corners.' Julie's mother stands in her dressing gown and pearls, and frowns at the Home Helper list of instructions. 'Agnes makes beds so beautifully. She could show you.'

Julie's stares with anger at the knot of sheets on her parents' bed. How is she supposed to make a whole lot of beds the proper way if her own mother can't show her how it's done? And how are you supposed to make your parents' bed when your mother is always sleeping in it! It's all so unfair and Julie is itching to pick up the phone and call the Pringles and ask if they might come and fetch her so she might be in a pleasant place on a Sunday, for no way would the Pringles have all those greasy frying-pans in the sink when Agnes is off and mothers yawning and frowning in dressing gowns that they wear all day every day while fathers show houses in their suburb of Plumstead, which he calls Lower Constantia when he's working. Where is Lower Constantia? Julie wants to know. How low does it go? It's not real her father says and her mother says yes it is, Lower Constantia absolutely exists as distinct from Plumstead, but Julie's father just laughs when they have this conversation. And when Julie asks again how low, he says all the way down, my girl, all the way ...

If she were Tracy-Ann, she wouldn't have to ask such questions of course, because she would live in Constantia-Constantia and live a Pringle kind of life with Charlene and Mike who neither frown nor wander nor oversleep, who help you with everything and answer things before you ask like what is a hospital corner, and this is why all the Pringles are so happy and good-looking and good at everything, this is why Tracy-Ann is a top Brownie, because her parents know what they are doing, they are running a tight ship. That's what Brown Owl would say. She often talks about ships in the powwows, about everyone being on board and working together to get somewhere. She likes *all hands on deck*. She likes *charting courses*. Sometimes they might even play the ship game when the Owl is in an energetic mood. Port! Starboard! The Brownies run from one side of the hall to the other as the Owl calls out the words, but Julie often gets her directions mixed up. She runs to starboard when she should be at port, and this means she must sit out the round and watch.

Julie leaves the bed sheets in a hump and stomps out of the room. She sees an angry sea and a leaky boat, her father smoking and stabbing at the air with the tip of his cigarette. 'Bit of a storm there if you ask me,' he says, as the sea washes in.

Lend a Hand

'Hey, Agnes, can you show me something?' Julie doesn't even have her school satchel off her shoulder yet. Agnes is in the kitchen wiping pots with a *lappie*.

'Wait,' Agnes says. 'I'm busy.'

'Come on, man,' Julie begs. She pulls Agnes by the arm. 'I've been waiting for you all weekend. You must come quickly.'

In Julie's room Agnes does not see an emergency and wants to know why she must come up? The room is neat and clean. Agnes has cleaned it as usual, making the bed, dusting and hanging up the clothes. Julie pulls the bed sheets into a mess and asks Agnes to start again, to do it nicely while she watches, but Agnes gets cross and says 'Who do you think you are? You are just a little girl, you are not my madam.'

Agnes is so cross she doesn't even wait for Julie to explain; she has already gone and called Julie's mom and is telling her that Julie is being very naughty and by the time Julie's mom gets up from her afternoon snooze and comes into the room, Julie is crying. 'I am not a naughty girl!' she shouts at Agnes. She feels slightly scared of Agnes because Agnes hardly ever gets cross, she is a very quiet kind of maid, but now she is shaking her head and has even said some words in Xhosa, which is always a bad sign.

'I think she just needs your help, Agnes,' Julie's mom says. 'Don't you, lovey? Tell Agnes nicely what you would like her to show you.'

But for some reason Julie can't ask Agnes to show her how to make the bed. She is frightened by the way Agnes became so angry with her so fast. Julie's dad has said Agnes can be cheeky when she's not getting things her way, but Julie does not understand why Agnes is so extremely angry about the bed even now while Julie's mom has explained the story behind what Julie wants. Except that even her mother doesn't know what Julie really wants, that she needs to get this badge so she will not lose her seat on the Pringle microbus and can continue to speed away after Brownies with her very best friend, up and away to Constantia-Constantia forever. But how do you explain this to your mother? At this rate, Julie thinks, I will never learn hospital corners.

The Brownie Smile

'We could use some help in defeating these Boers,' Julie says. 'Let's round up all the young boys and use them as messengers in this war so that we may triumph in this Siege of Mafeking. Yes!' Julie claps her hands together. 'Let boys join the effort. We should not shelter our children. We should teach them to be brave. For the sake of England and her Queen. For her African land!'

Julie finished her lines in the deep booming voice she has chosen and looks around at her fellow tortoises for approval. Everyone seems to think she is very convincing as Lord Baden-Powell, the inventor of the Cub Scouts. Julie folds her script, puts it down on the bare wood floor of the Brownie hall. For the first time as a Brownie, Julie is enjoying herself.

When she speaks her lines, she feels as if there is a smile inside her stomach, twisting and settling. The Pack Away play night is going to be a hit, especially the tortoise part. The Brownies are to perform the history of Brownies; each six has been given a summary of a section of the story. It is up to them to research their piece of the story and find ways to present their bit well, so that on performance night, the other Brownies will all be entertained and the full history of the Cub Scouts, Girl Guides, and Brownies will reveal itself in front of the campfire.

Julie looks at the rest of her tortoise six with new eyes, with the sort of fondness she feels for real tortoises. The tortoises are not clever or interesting, but they chose her to be Lord Baden-Powell and Julie is grateful. Something about pretending to be the man makes her calm and excited at the same time. When she is Baden-Powell she can forget about the problems of Home Helper, forget about unmade beds and all those dishes she could never hope to do in time for the awards ceremony. Dishes and beds and homes are not important to Baden-Powell. He is focused on trenches and tents and striding up and down in the bush with binoculars looking for the Afrikaner enemy.

Julie loves thinking about this play, about the way in which Brownies came to be, inspired by the great Baden-Powell, a brave and good man who made children important. She has seen pictures of Baden-Powell. He has a wide beige moustache, and a big head with a hard white hat like a shell. She has only seen a picture of him from the chest up, but Julie feels she has seen the whole of him. He has hairless Mike Pringly shiny legs in khaki shorts and a large African walking-stick. He has goldy skin, brown muscular arms, and very red, Pringly lips. Julie cannot wait to be Baden-Powell in Buinskloof – just two weekends away – waving his stick at all the Brownies and telling them what is what. And though she doesn't know quite how yet, she knows that on the night of the performance she is going to do something extra, something to make her Baden-Powell stand out and be a crowd-pleaser so those Brownies and Owls see her with new eyes.

And who knows, maybe Brown Owl will be so moved she might even slap on an extra badge, the Drama Bug, with its cute little happy and sad masks their upturned and down-turned mouths stitching tears and laughter in gold embroidery down Julie's arm ...

Julie wanders off for a drink of water, or at least that's what she says. Mostly she wants to eavesdrop on the bush babies, on Tracy-Ann and her group to see how their acting is going. She passes by and hears Tracy-Ann, her voice high and whiny. Tracy-Ann is meant to be Juliette 'Daisy' Gordon-Low, the lady who invented Girl Scouts and Brownies after meeting Baden-Powell, Daisy who went deaf because she got a grain of rice stuck in her ear on her wedding day.

Passing Tracy, Julie hears a feeble Daisy voice. It's a little bit shocking to hear Tracy-Ann being bad at something, but Julie figures it's because Tracy-Ann is so good and successful at being herself she can't be good at being someone else.

Home Helper. First-Year Star. And Baden-Powell. Pack Away camp is going to make Julie into a successful Brownie! And as Tracy-Ann shakes her head to get the imaginary rice grain out of her ear, Julie is happy. Sometimes even a tortoise is better than a bush baby.

The Friendship Squeeze

'Not this weekend,' Tracy-Ann says at school. 'Sorry.'

Julie is dumbfounded. The metal taste of her Marmite sandwich rises at the back of her throat. What? No Saturday after-Brownies playing at the Pringle house? No lolling on the golf grass, no making doll's house dustbins from thimbles? Why?

Home Helper

Tracy-Ann's not telling. She doesn't seem cross, but there is a tight and pinchy look in her face, a sad secret hidden in her skin. It takes a moment, but when Tracy-Ann turns away and glides up to the classroom, Julie knows.

She knows that Tracy-Ann knows.

Tracy-Ann knows Julie isn't truly earning her Home Helper badge, she knows Julie has been lying through her teeth from the beginning and that no amount of bed-making since her lie is enough, because a whole month of beds, dishes, laundry, one-cent pieces and cooking an entire family meal is too much, so Julie's parents are helping her fib, fudging numbers of beds and plates, adding their signatures to lists of things that never got folded or cleaned up, at least not by Julie. Tracy-Ann is not stupid. Julie has broken her Promise. She is not doing her best. And it makes Tracy-Ann sad.

Julie gets sweaty. She is amazed at herself. All that wasted time, all that wandering around as if your own best friend doesn't have choices of her own she could make, and why shouldn't she when she's on a Highway and you are way behind on a Footpath lying to keep up, why shouldn't she give you up? And something much worse occurs to Julie. Didn't Mike and Charlene seem slightly sad too, last Saturday? Wasn't there something a little bit funny in the air when Julie went over to play?

She sees Mike and Charlene looking sorrowful but firm as they sit with Tracy-Ann in the kitchen, having a heart-to-heart. Maybe they are saying the kind of things Brown Owl says to the circle – that the road of life is about choosing right from wrong and staying on your path. Maybe once they encouraged Tracy-Ann to take pity on those less fortunate than ourselves in Plumstead. But maybe now they are saying that other Brown Owl thing, that one about helping those who help themselves, not helping those who cheat.

The bell rings. Is it too late, Julie wonders, to find a way out? This is the last weekend before the Buinskloof camp and badge ceremony. What would be the right path to choose now? Let the lie stand and hope that with the new neat square on her sleeve she will look better and the Pringles can forget how the badge got there and just admire the sleeve instead, its gold house-shaped stitching? Or would it be better to confess right there in the circle, tell everyone what happened, fall down in front of the toadstool and ask for forgiveness and a second chance? *I promise to do my best. To . . .*

Julie is getting carried away. Tracy-Ann couldn't know about the lie, she decides. Tracy-Ann's pinchy hiding look and the cancelled weekend playing can't have anything to do with Home Helper. The secret must be simpler than that: Mike and Charlene sadly sitting at the kitchen table talking about goals and thinking of Julie's parents in their badly paved Plumstead driveway, their Plumstead faces as blank and unfriendly as walls. *Tracy, the road of life requires good paving.* Wouldn't it be nice for Tracy-Ann to widen her friendship circle, invite a new Brownie home for a change?

A Good Turn

Now that Julie knows whose fault it is she has a sudden, new focus. She no longer has the wandering feeling. Her plan is complicated, but she is going to get really organised and do it all. She is going to fix things up.

She assesses the Home Helper list. She has enough signatures next to the drawings of beds and dishes, but there are other things besides signatures that she needs, things she must give to Brown Owl. And there are only six days left.

Julie shakes the HeavenCent-A-Day piggy bank at the dining room table. Its nearly hollow belly gives off a pathetic rattle, as if someone had already emptied it and accidentally left coins in. With a pang for the Pringles Julie realises she has neglected the poor. The truth is that neither Julie nor anyone else in the family has made their contribution more than a couple of times. It all went wrong very fast. Julie's dad had said a few coppers are meaningless and on day three he tried to put in a shiny fifty cents, but it was too big for the slot, and Julie got cross when he slid in some smaller silver coins. The cents are supposed to show a daily thought, she explained, and putting other coins in goes against the rules – it is not on the list and anyway, Brown Owl says it all adds up in the end, and most important, it's the thought that counts. The thought that counts? Julie's dad laughed. Tell that to the guy in the shack! And that was the end of that.

So the pig is empty. But never mind, Julie thinks. She is clear and sharp.

She is clear on the business of Izaan, that while Tracy-Ann got into the microbus on her own yesterday after Brownies, Izaan Strauss surely got driven to Tracy-Ann's house. Mike Pringle must have told Tracy-Ann it would be horrible to hurt Julie's feelings by giving Izaan Strauss a lift, but Julie isn't stupid, and that's why she must now work extra hard. This knowledge pushes her each night at bedtime as she reads and rereads the Baden-Powell speech that she has written and researched herself. This is also a part of the plan. She knows that a perfectly memorised part on Pack Away performance night will show Tracy-Ann and everyone else. That plus Home Helper will seal the deal.

'Loose change.' She bears down on her father in passages and doorways, in the lounge and in the car on her way to school. She demands money and her father says what's this, highway robbery in my own house? But there's never enough loose change, never enough one cents.

'Bank,' Julie barks at her father. He pretends to be annoyed, but he laughs and promises anyway, and she knows at the end of the week he will produce rolls of one-cent pieces and wave them around on Friday, saying okay little missionary, here's your gift from God.

The final chore in her notebook – clothing collection – is easy. Julie slinks around bathrooms and bedrooms after supper and before school, snatching from dark cupboards – old holey tracksuit trousers, Woolworths jerseys, it doesn't matter what, only how much. Late Friday night she pauses in her parents' doorway waiting to hear their regular sleep breaths before she can steal in and pick up what she wants most of all. And when she darts out, thrusting it into the black plastic bag in her hands, she feels the pleasure of accomplishment. She is finally—as the tortoise song says she must –*helping others in a fix*. And she's also helping herself. Which feels at least two steps up from the usual tortoise tea-cosy work.

The Path

Sun streams through the house in yellow blocks, so much sun that Julie feels sick. She has been up since the deep blue of early morning, packing her camp kitbag, making and re-making her bed, and cleaning cleaning cleaning because today, Saturday, she cannot leave anything for Agnes. Today she is leaving home for camp and bringing the Home Helper proof to Brown Owl. But Home Helper has nothing to do with why she is cleaning. Julie is cleaning because the Pringle microbus is arriving in thirty minutes. Once again, it's coming to pick Julie up, and even if the Pringles do not approve of Julie anymore, they would not leave her behind, not today of all days, when the Buinskloof camp begins and Mr – and *Mike* – Pringle is one of the camp drivers.

Julie has swept the kitchen floor of crumbs and dried peas. She has mopped the dark entrance hall and pushed coats into cupboards. Everything looks good. Her father will look good because he has a show house and will be in a suit. And her mother will have no choice but to put something on, some proper clothes, and come downstairs. Julie has made sure of that and she knows that her mother is getting the message, thudding around in her room saying 'It's always hanging on the door, I just don't understand where it has gone.'

But she will understand, Julie thinks as she makes coffee for the first time in her life, turning on the kettle. Her mother will understand soon enough and she will also have to come down to say goodbye, she will have to come down in clothes and have coffee with Mike, who himself will understand over coffee with Julie's nicely dressed parents in their clean kitchen, that Julie is okay, that she is not a Pringle but she is doing her best and the house isn't so bad on the inside, not so bad after all. And while Mike is finding this out, Julie will make sure that Tracy-Ann has seen her neatly made bed and spotless room and then Tracy-Ann will look at Julie with the look of a Brownie and a best friend and everything will be the way it used to be with Julie back on that Pringle lawn by next week.

But Mike is late and he looks like he has just woken up himself. His hair is shooting off in different directions, he has bits of white dry spit in the corners of his mouth, and Julie is slightly embarrassed to see him this way, with his hair all spiky and a crusty morning mouth. With her own father this sort of thing is to be expected. But with Mike Pringle it feels somehow rude, something you shouldn't see. Like watching him on the loo. Julie looks away. Mike apologises: there is not time for coffee, there is not even time even for Tracy-Ann to get out of the car. Julie shouts to her mother to come down, but her mother says I'm not dressed and would you come up to say goodbye, darling.

Mike heaves Julie's kitbag and into the microbus boot. Julie stands in front of her front door. Mike comes back to the door get her black plastic bag of Home Helper donation clothes. 'Have you said your goodbyes?' he asks her.

She stands and blinks. They haven't even left, but already everything has gone wrong.

The Vow

Things are worse at the Brownie hall. Julie hands Brown Owl the clothes for the poor and the signed Home Helper book, so that Brown Owl can lock everything away and know to take a Home

Helper badge to Buinskloof for Julie during the badge ceremony. But where is the money for Julie's HeavenCent-A-Day contribution? An egg grows in Julie's throat. A large hard egg. She has forgotten! She has forgotten to get the money from her father, and in forgetting, she has paid for not saying goodbye to her parents and for lying to Mr Pringle about it. Julie stares at Brown Owl's chin flap. She knows the only right path now is the wrong one.

'I have it,' she lies to Brown Owl. 'Right next to my bed. It's full. I just forgot it. Please Brown Owl,' she begs. 'Can I get the badge anyway?' But Brown Owl tells her that she has a lesson to learn, one cannot simply have the badge on one's sleeve without completing one's tasks. And so one cannot remain a privileged visitor at a particular Brownie's home. Julie hears this beneath Brown Owl's words — that a Brownie must always Be Prepared, for that is the motto and if one is not properly ready in one's life one cannot expect to be rewarded by a Pringle kind of life. There has to be a forfeit.

Julie begs Brown Owl. She swears on her Brownie Honour she will fetch the money immediately on return from camp. Tracy-Ann is across the room. Julie looks past Brown Owl at Tracy-Ann's remote eyes and she sees a sign of the future: Julie's one-year Brownie anniversary will mark the end of everything. She can see it quite clearly, the way the world tumbles and slips away at the Owls' first sighting of her empty sleeve. 'What kind of Brownie are you?' they will want to know. 'What have you ever done for anyone?'

Pack Away

'Girls, be sure you are ready to perform at seven tonight,' Brown Owl says. They are having an outside powwow. Julie's bottom is chilly, as though she has something extra growing on it. The ground is damp and the air is a bleary grey at Buinskloof, the river noisy and dark with early winter. But Julie doesn't mind. She smiles at Brown Owl, for Brown Owl has agreed to give her the Home Helper badge after all, she is letting Julie stay on her path provided the piggy bank be given back to Brown Owl within one week. Julie is fine with promising this, and she is fine with most anything, she was even fine with the fact that there was no room for her in the Pringle microbus on the way to Buinskloof because the bus was full up with bush babies so Julie and the rest of the tortoises had to go in the Brownie bus with the duikers, with Izaan Strauss in the front seat and Tawny Owl driving, Izaan playing her recorder the whole way there.

But Julie feels very good about everything, even the fact that she can't share the dorm with Tracy-Ann – that the bush babies have to room with the dassies. She doesn't mind because this time tomorrow the badge will be hers and Tracy-Ann will stop being sad and complicated and quiet, she will stop being those things even sooner when she sees Julie's Baden-Powell performance in only a few hours.

Baden-Powell at the campfire!

Marshmallows after!

Julie gets a powwow at the thought. She has her costume ready, the khaki shorts and socks, the walking-stick, the false moustache. She has memorised the lines she wrote and thrown in a few extra. Because of this night Julie doesn't even mind the food they have to eat, the egg sandwiches for lunch. She doesn't even mind the spaghetti that will be made in the main hut this evening. She has seen the giant metal pot filled with red slosh tomato and it was bad, but not bad enough to make her feel bad.

'And we will have a guest audience tonight,' Brown Owl continued her announcements. 'Brownie Troop 122 of Parow North will be joining us around the campfire for the play.' Julie's throat is tight and coated with hardness as though she swallowed a straw and it got stuck on the way. The rest of the day, its meals and songs, its leadership games and mountain walk, all merge together and flow past like a river until the end actually gets there. The fire. The visiting Brownie pack arriving from their bungalows further down the camp. There is tea. There are marshmallows, their scented paleness strange, the taste so particular and heavy that Julie feels almost revolted even as she reached to stuff more into her mouth. Marshmallows are hardly ever around. At least not at Julie's house.

And the play arrives, after all these weeks and this whole long day, the play is here.

Tawny Owl announces the first pack on, in order of historical events. The dassies begin and pretend to be Boers and English, pretend to fight each other and they do it badly and boringly, and now it's Julie up there and everyone is looking at her and clapping, the visiting Brownies too, dark faces with flickers of red from the fire. There is a little fire in Julie's own tummy as her voice fills the fierce air and the wind smacks her kneecaps, exposed and red in the pale shorts of Baden-Powell. When she walks around the circle twirling her big moustache, even Brown Owl laughs.

'We could use some help defeating these Boers.' Julie says her words as if each is a round ripe peach that she has plucked off a tree. Her voice is a command and the audience, after the soft whispery stage mewls of dassies, sits and listens. And now Julie fully understands what it means to do something for others. She wants to give them more than just her scripted words. She wants to give them everything she's got, make them laugh, make them remember her forever, not just Tracy-Ann but all of them, all the Brownies in the world.

'We've got to nail those Afrikaners.' Julie improvises to make her words more powerful. 'Get the Dutchmen out of here!' she adds. From the circle around her, she hears some laughter and it pushes her on. 'Let's blast those crunchies to high heaven!' She shouts in a posh, hot-potato Brown Owl sort of accent and now there's a lot of laughter because she used that silly funny word, and she is sure she can hear Tracy-Ann hysterical, even the Owls are smiling at the rudeness of it.

'Let's get our boys involved!' Baden-Powell continues, striding back and forth around the campfire, his long socks perfectly pulled up around his nut-brown hairless legs as he shakes his finger at the tortoise troops gathered to listen to his command. 'Let's push those Boers out of the bush!' He stands, rooted to history, to the earth below his feet, God watching from above. Everyone loves him, loves his ideas. He now knows that when he was born nobody noticed, but when he dies the world won't forget.

There is clapping when Julie finishes her speech, but when she bows and looks up, when she is Julie again, she worries that maybe some of the Parow North visiting troop are Afrikaans and that their feelings are hurt. They don't seem to be clapping as hard. Most of them look black to Julie, but maybe they're coloured. If they are black, they would speak Xhosa, she concludes and they would hate the crunchies just as much as Baden-Powell, maybe more. They would be clapping like mad if they were. But didn't her father say there's no such thing as a black Brownie? And if they are coloured they would probably speak Afrikaans, Julie knows that. Except don't coloureds hate the Afrikaners?

She is confused. In this light, it's too hard to see what those Brownies are and even in the day sometimes coloureds can be so dark you can't tell. Or so light you can't tell. And even when they speak you can't always tell either what they are, they might be Englishy sort of coloureds with *klonkie* accents because they live in *grakkie* lower-class places like Parow, which is so much lower than even Lower Constantia. Why is it all so unclear?

But one thing is, at least, very clear: Izaan Strauss is offended, her arms folded across her chest. Julie definitely couldn't care less if she has offended Izaan. That would be a bonus prize, because if Izaan knows that Brownies were born to get rid of Afrikaners in the first place, maybe she wouldn't strut around quite so much and instead feel grateful that people like Julie and Tracy-Ann even let her in the Fernwood pack at all!

Yes, Julie thinks, bowing again and returning to sit in the audience. Afrikaners should be grateful they are even allowed to play the recorder in a Brownie pack. But Julie has a sour taste in her mouth, a feeling worse than lying, a feeling she has done something really wrong, forgotten something really important because Tracy-Ann is up on stage and suddenly she doesn't want to act, says she doesn't feel well, is walking off stage and Tawny has her arm around Tracy's shoulders and now it all makes sense, what Julie has forgotten.

Tracy's mother! Her name, *Charlene*. And all the other clues: a judge in the Bokomo Baking competition, that dark-skin-green-eyed-certain-sort-of-look. These are small things but things Julie should know, did once even know – these are signs of being Afrikaans. Even though her voice is soft and not very crunchie at all, Julie can't believe that Charlene's Charleneness slipped her mind. Her own mother has even said it when commenting on her when Tracy-Ann first came to Julie's school. *Anglo-Afrikaner*. The ones who do not live in Durbanville. The ones who know to avoid face-brick on their houses. Whose husbands or wives are English. But they can never truly pass, Julie's mother explained. You can always tell. The kind of haircuts they give their sons. And even if they speak nicely most of the time, they still say *sies* and *come with*. Charlene Pringle. Why can't Julie ever focus?

As the bush babies fumble around trying to tell Daisy Low's bit of history without Tracy-Ann, Julie sits in the dark. She can't understand how it is she can know things and yet not know them at the same time. But everything gets so muddy, so complicated, with Afrikaans people in Constantia speaking English ... could she not say that to Tracy-Ann by way of excusing herself? Won't Tracy forgive her?

Bad luck. Julie blames bad luck. Why couldn't she have got to be Daisy Low instead, the Girl Guide American lady? If she had been deaf Daisy she could have amused Tracy, which is all she really wanted to do, which was the main point in the first place. Daisy Low, with the rice grain in her ear, that could have been so fun to act. And Tracy-Ann with her two good ears would have laughed and laughed and cheered but now she is gone from the ring and Julie is alone and later, in her bunk, after Tracy-Ann has refused to speak to her, Julie will lie there and for the first time she is away from her parents, and she should be happy, this should be exactly where she wants to be, where she has wanted to be for a long time. But instead she thinks of bad luck Baden-Powell and wishes he had never been born. She is glad he's dead, but it doesn't help her now. He was right: the whole world would remember him forever, especially Julie of the Fernwood tortoise six.

Road and Highway

'Let's have a song, Izaan,' Mike suggests. He is behind the wheel of his microbus and they are speeding away down the N2 home to Cape Town from the camp. For once, Julie wishes she wasn't put in this Pringle microbus with Tracy-Ann; however, Tawny had rearranged the home lifts and put Julie in with Tracy-Ann and Izaan.

Izaan plays 'I Zigga Zoomba' on her recorder and the girls in the bus start to sing, but Tracy-Ann in the front seat keeps her mouth shut and her eyes on the road ahead. Tracy-Ann has barely spoken to Julie since the play, and she wasn't even at the court of awards when Julie received her Home Helper – she was sick in her dorm or at least that's what she told everyone, that she had a headache and didn't feel like doing anything. The Owls fussed around her for this was so unlike Tracy-Ann, but Julie avoided her. She didn't want to hear Tracy say that she didn't like seeing Julie make fun of her mother. She didn't want Tracy to look at her and say 'What kind of friend are you?'

I-zigga-zoomba-zoomba-zoomba, I-zigga-zoomba-zoomba zay. The sky is the colour of hot metal. In the distance Table Mountain is as blue as a summer plum and its famous tabletop shape isn't there, not yet at least because the road has to curve first before the mountain turns and angles itself into its line, the flat long top with Devil's Peak on its left hand side, Devil's Peak always a bit scary to

Julie, always a bit not right. She hears her father's word. Not right, but left. *Sinistra*.

She stuffs her mouth full of pink marshmallows. She has eaten ten already today, plus three cream soda fizzers and three strawberry, but she can't stop. She won a whole bag of sweets with the tortoises during a stepping-stone exercise next to the river, but Helen Curtain, another tortoise, didn't want her marshmallows so Julie got double. She stuffs them in. Her stomach tightens and she sees the mountain turn and change, the richness coating her insides with a clammy pink, like a sticky hand gripping her from the inside out. And she sees her mother's face in Lower Constantia, waiting for her, and the uneven paving of her driveway. The other girls sing, in rounds, and the alternating lines mix and tumble and make Julie dizzy. *Hold them down, you Zulu warrior. Hold them – hold them down. Down.*

Julie wants to say she is sorry to Tracy-Ann, and she is sorry, but she can only stare into the white light of the sun shining off bits of broken glass near the airport. Shacks flick by, reflecting the sun back at itself and at Julie, a million bright roofs that hurt her head. There is another deep sorry feeling in her stomach somewhere next to all the bubbling pink. She tries to name the feeling but she doesn't know what it is, she has never felt it before. And now it is rising, thick in her throat.

'Can you stop the car?' she mumbles to Mike. *Hold them down, you Zulu warrior.* 'Stop the car,' she repeats. *Hold them down, you Zulu chief chief chief,* but Julie doesn't think she can hold it down a second longer and before Mike has even properly pulled off the road, Julie runs from the car and into the bushes beside the airport road.

Into the bush, she vomits a stream of bright spongey spit, its haunting sweet sickness will live beneath her lips for days to come, the pink pool at her feet a surprise, something she never knew was in her but now is clear and shocking. She is sick. She is homesick.

There is a rustle. Julie pulls herself up. Someone is watching her. He steps out from the bushes, white clay paint on his face. An amaKwetha. They stare at each other. Julie has seen them often, the amaKwethas on the airport road, teenage Xhosa boys doing their rite of passage, living in huts alone away from their families to show they are grown-ups. Julie wipes her mouth, steps back over torn thorn bushes, snagged rubbish bags, watching the amaKwetha. He is half naked and has white clay on his body and old *takkies* on his feet. She has always liked spotting these boy-men from the car, like they were a lucky charm, like they were a good I-Spy sighting, a blinking second of white face as the car whipped past. Up close it is not the same. Up close they watch you back.

The amaKwetha looks at the pink vomit on the dust and walks away.

Quiet Sign

Tracy-Ann is not at Brownies the following week, nor the one after. She seems to avoid Julie at school too. She doesn't say much and Julie bides her time too, avoiding Tracy-Ann. She is afraid saying sorry won't be enough, but if she doesn't say it, it still holds the promise of being enough. If she doesn't say it, it might still work when she does.

'I'm busy,' Tracy-Ann says when Julie asks her during small break why she hasn't been coming to Brownies.

At home, Julie wonders out loud to her parents even though she knows they won't have anything helpful to say. Her father never has anything helpful to say, like when Julie told him about the coloured Brownies from Parow and didn't most coloureds speak Afrikaans? Her father laughed and said if they speak Xhosa then they're blackies not brownies, man, and I don't care what costume they're wearing.

And when Tracy-Ann goes on not arriving at Brownies Julie thinks maybe now she has ruined Brownies for Tracy-Ann too. She writes a proper apology, puts it on Tracy's desk on Thursday at school. Except Tracy doesn't come to school that day.

'Their house is on the market,' her father tells her that night. 'A low price. A price more fit for Lower Constantia.' Julie puts her fork and knife neatly together on her plate although she has not finished her food. Even though she is about to get her First-Year Star, even though the little gold star shape is waiting to go onto her sleeve in a matter of days, she knows the good part of Brownies is gone.

'I miss my old dressing-gown,' her mother says. 'I still don't know where it went.'

The Grand Salute

After Tracy-Ann moved away, she sent Julie a postcard from Port Elizabeth. She couldn't explain properly because it was private, but they had to move, she said. Back to the Eastern Cape where they were from. She was sorry she didn't say goodbye. She said she thought Julie was a good Baden-Powell. That she was sorry she felt too sick to say so at the time.

Other children talked at school. Mr Pringle had lost all his money. Someone's mother was on the board at Kirstenbosch and someone else's mother did flowers with Mr Pringle for school events. They all knew things that Julie had never heard of. Odd words floated around. *Embezzling*. Things to do with Mr Pringle and getting too rich from the chain of Stirrups steak houses he owned. Things to do with the government and breaking the law. Julie was shocked and confused about Mike, but even more than that she felt a deep relief she wasn't in trouble for talking about crunchies as Baden-Powell. Embezzling, whatever that was, could not be as bad as if Tracy-Ann really hated her for being mean.

Still, embezzling was a bad-sounding word and it sounded so completely out of place in a Pringle life, as wrong and out of place as if some amaKwetha just showed up and decided to set up his ritual hut on the Pringle tennis court.

Julie asks her parents about embezzling. They are in the car on the way to Brownies where Julie will get her First-Year Star. 'And why did Mike put his money in the laundry anyway?' Julie asks. Victoria Clarke's mother had said something about this *laundry* business, making Julie worry for Mike and all the Pringles. She knows the government is bad and cruel, her parents always say so, but she didn't know they could really punish you for laundering your own rand in the machine!

'It refers to stealing. Stealing and lying,' her mother says in a high, queenly voice. 'Mr Pringle evidently stole and lied.'

Julie's father takes a different road, up into the high wide curves of Constantia, winding shady loops lined with oaks. He slows down near the Pringle house.

Julie watches as the tennis court peeps from the back of the house, a new green concrete rectangle fresh and unused. She heard that the government came for everything, cleared the Pringles out. *Repossession*. Took even the forks and knives from their kitchen. She wonders whether they took the doll's house too, carried off its miniature forks and knives. Without its minty curtains and covered pelmets visible in the big windows the house looks empty, its windows nude. But at least the lawn is still there, as green as a golf course and grown in now; you could no longer see its roll-on lines.

Julie stares into the grass as her parents argue about the Pringles, her dad saying *Ag*, it means nothing, and come on, since when did cooking the books become such a crime in this place? He points his cigarette at the house. Yes the man was a bit dodgy and definitely a bit precious but poor bugger, now he's probably living in some *storrosh*. Shame! Even *my* heart is bleeding a bit of lumpy custard.

Stealing and lying. Julie still can't believe this of Mike. A worthy man. That's what her teacher had called him. She says it out loud in the car, but now that word sounds as hollow as the house looks and her father says I don't know about that and I always knew there was something *sinistra* going on. Still, poor oke, man.

Julie's mother sighs, touching the pearls at her neck. The Pringles' dark roof flashes with sun. Julie thinks of Charlene and her perfume smell, and the way she had winked at Julie during the baking competition and pronounced her scones to be very nice even though they were as flat as pancakes. She looks at the house and then at the HeavenCent-A-Day piggy bank on the seat next to her, which she still has not given to Brown Owl, the piggy bank hollow until this morning when her dad unloaded the bankrolls of one-cent-pieces into its slot. This is absolutely your last chance, Julie, says Brown Owl, chin jiggling. If it's not here next week you will forfeit your star.

Julie thinks of her own lies and of whether she actually stole her Home Helper badge. She also feels confused about the piggy bank. Would it have made her a better person to cheat with rolls of coins to help the poor or give the piggy bank back to Brown Owl and tell the truth, tell her that they don't much care about any of this business, that Julie is a Brownie for other reasons?

She wonders if all of this makes her as bad as a Mike Pringle because she is just a child and surely if she starts now she will only get worse. She broke her Promise. She didn't choose right from wrong. She never kept the Brownie law, not even for her first year. Considering all the wrong things she did, she should be extra happy to think of the one badge she actually did earn, the First-Year Star. It is the only badge she deserves because she may have broken all the laws but she has been a Brownie for a year. She has shown up and no one can say any different, even if Brown Owl didn't give it, it would still be hers.

Except getting badges is not the same without Tracy-Ann there, without Tracy getting more badges to add to her sleeve of badges, a new picture to add to all the other pictures. House, fire, ball, rope, music note. The gold-thread mermaid for Water Baby. Without Tracy-Ann, without Mike, really everything is gone.

The house swims in Julie's eyes and she has that wandering feeling again, that feeling of never being in one place, of never being able to stay somewhere long enough. Nothing is still, not even houses.

Almost a First-Year Star. Almost a year of showing up, but this time she knows she can't.

Julie cries. Her father pats her leg and says it's a nice house, a gracious Constantia home. She keeps crying, and her mom is speaking too, saying a lovely, worthy house. And the Pringles had a super time in it, didn't they?

MAKHOSAZANA XABA

Running

I'm a runner. That's the role I've given myself. A sub-role if you like. I run from the plenary room to the small groups rooms, to prepare them. I run from these rooms to the office to fetch and deliver messages and requests. I take children from the playroom to their mothers, and vice versa (there are three toddlers and one on the breast). I run to call for technical help, something we seem to need often. Even the electricity in this hotel has its own mind. I run from the conference venue to our makeshift office, my hotel room, when we need to replenish stock. Yesterday I ran my way into a taxi: we drove to the nearest chemist to get anti-allergy medication after a comrade reacted to no one knows what. The doctor said my running made a big difference.

As a team we call ourselves the AST, for 'administrative support team'. There are five of us. I feel privileged to be working with such women – accomplished in their professions, steeped in the organisation's politics, respected, women of integrity. All of them much older than I, in their forties and fifties. That's why I chose to do the running bit; they are not as quick on their feet as they are with their brains. I have learned so much in just a week of preparations. I was asked to join the AST for this conference when a comrade fell sick.

This conference. Well, this conference is history in the making. As an AST we are the mechanics. We are the oil, the nuts and bolts of the train to liberation. We've been talking in the team about the potential historical significance of this conference. Who knows, maybe ten years from today South Africa will be free. MK, the people's army, will have struck a heavy blow to the apartheid regime, freeing the country. Freeing us all.

I suspect the leadership is hiding certain facts. Why have they started preparing a constitution? They know something we soldiers don't. Maybe freedom is closer than we can ever imagine. What with all these delegations from South Africa we keep hearing are arriving in Lusaka, holding secret meetings with the leadership and returning home. We are at the brink of something. Something significant. I can feel it.

That's the other reason I'm so proud to be part of this conference. As a soldier you don't get to hear much. The camps are claustrophobic. Here in the Zambian capital news flows. I doubt the leadership likes that.

I've become a civilian. I'm a bit conflicted by that, actually, because as a trained soldier of the people's army I should be with the other soldiers, preparing for a military takeover. Besides, there are so few women soldiers. I love the action, the discipline, the precision, the myriad skills, the versatility. Being a soldier means a lot more, is a lot more. Philosophically speaking, everyone in this movement matters, plays a key role. But, hey, for me the underground army is it.

My running role at this conference is synonymous with that of a soldier. But, being a soldier at a women's conference is unique. I'm moving between the two pillars of our struggle, mass political mobilisation and armed struggle. This conference brings in another dimension, the international mobilisation, and I am a part of it. When I think of it this way, my conflict fades away.

The women of the ANC decided to revise the draft constitution in order to make it non-sexist. That's why we are all here, one hundred and twenty of us, and only fifteen men. Seeing all these women in the flesh, in one place, made my pores sing a love song for my country. The names on the registration forms are now bodies I can touch. When I heard everyone introduce themselves yesterday during the opening session I was humbled. It was a pleasant surprise to hear where they have all come from, the work they do for the ANC in all those countries. With such an ocean of experience we have a right to call ourselves the 'government in waiting'.

Yesterday went much better than I expected. I ran from morning till late in the evening. I'm very disappointed by the service we're getting from this hotel. They're riding on the wave of long-lost fame. I can't deal with such inefficiency. The conference venue is far from the hotel's administrative office; so I find myself running up and down to get the support we need from them.

At the end of the day, the AST came together for evaluation and prepared a summary of the day's proceedings. We smoothed the administrative glitches by meeting with the hotel management. Nomazwi, our team leader, was so direct with them I know today will be better.

At 7 AM sharp we arrive. The biggest room, named after President Kenneth Kaunda, is the main meeting room for the four days of this conference. For group work we have five smaller rooms named after Zambia's colonial masters, whose 'discovery' claims I know not.

Nomazwi is clear: 'We have to ensure the curtains are in their hooks before we draw them open for day two. That's what working behind the scenes is about.' We do our work with Nomazwi's guidance. Even with the improvements I still run a few errands before we start. When the delegates walk through the door we are ready at our table at the back of the plenary room. Conference starts promptly at 9 AM.

Today's agenda is more exciting than yesterday's. We are getting into the content details of non-sexism – the practical, more interesting things. Yesterday we focused on contextual issues, concepts I know well. I hope I'll be able to listen to some of the sessions. I want to listen to comrade Lungi from Washington. Her paper, 'Making Town Planning Non-sexist: a Model for the New South Africa', promises to be educational. It's the most unusual thing to choose to talk about. I'm curious. She is the first woman town planner I know.

I'm excited as we walk out for tea. Comrade Lungi is the first speaker after the tea break. When we are all back in the plenary session and comrade Mapule, the chairperson, introduces comrade Lungi, my anticipation heightens.

Someone taps me on the shoulder indicating with his head I need to step out. It's a man I now know well, hotel staff. I step out, closing the door as gently as he had opened it. Just behind to the door is comrade S'bu. He works in the Department of Information and Publicity.

'Comrade, I need to deliver an urgent message to all the conference delegates. Please tell the chairperson I need to interrupt.' I notice the piece of paper in his hands. It's shaking. I look into his eyes and know whatever it is, it's dead serious.

'Come, comrade.' I usher him into the plenary room. I bend over to tell Nomazwi what's happening. I beckon S'bu to come with me. We walk next to each other down the center of the room to the stage where two speakers and comrade Mapule are sitting.

'The fourth section is on spatial concepts and processes. Therein I assert that women's freedom is intricately interlinked with the physical spaces we constructed around us.'

Comrade Lungi flips the white cue card under the small pile in her left hand. I stare at her as I get closer to the stage. She has a black-and-white tailored suit made from kente fabric, an A-line skirt and a jacket. The white collar of her blouse reveals a slender neck, the colour of slightly toasted brown bread. As I get closer to the table I conclude she is beautiful. I suspect she is younger than me.

'In the fifth section I propose options for creating safe spaces for women and how to deal with homelessness. To do this I use examples mostly from the Scandinavian countries, where this has been achieved with varying degrees of success.'

My heart beats faster from a sense of agitation I don't understand. Walking next to comrade S'bu is making me anxious. I wonder if Lungi has children.

'The sixth section looks at my proposal for the movement. As you can imagine, comrades, I have very strong feelings about this.' She smiles as she says this. If she is disturbed by our approach she is not showing it.

We step up the three stairs onto the stage. I whisper into Mapule's ear while comrade S'bu stands right next to me. His left hand is now in his trouser pocket. His right hand still has the piece of paper.

'In the last section I conclude with some crucial remarks, pointers really. Pointers I would encourage you all to take into consideration as this historic conference proceeds.' Lungi looks at us, waits.

Comrade Mapule stands and addresses the delegates.

'Comrades, for those of you who have not met comrade S'bu, he is from our Information and Publicity Department based here in Lusaka. Please pardon the interruption, he is bringing urgent news.'

Mapule sits. Comrade Lungi follows suit. I squat at the end of the table. I've been squatting a lot during this conference when it's my turn to carry the roving mike for the open discussion sessions.

Comrade S'bu approaches the podium, his right fisted hand in the air. '*Amandla!*'

'*Awethu,*' resounds in this large plenary room.

'Comrades, I will not waste your time. I know you are discussing important issues of our movement. We decided it would be folly to delay the delivery of such news. The enemy has struck. Once again the enemy has struck.'

He pauses. An uncomfortable, long pause. He looks at the piece of paper in his hand and reads from it.

'This morning we received news from home. Comrade Reverend Vukile Dladla of the Methodist Church in Edendale, near Pietrmaritzburg, in Natal, was gunned down this morning at about 7 AM. He was in his car. He had just finished an early morning meeting with comrades in the church. He died on the seat of his car. Five bullets were found in his body. Three were lodged in his head.'

Silence. Then voices begin to murmur. How did they get the news so fast? Damn, these comrades are impressive! My head begins to spin.

'Comrades, once again we are reminded that the struggle continues. Comrade Reverend Vukile Dladla's death should be an inspiration to us all. His death is not vain. His death *cannot* be in vain. The blood that was spilled this morning should remind us that the enemy is not sleeping. *Amandla*!' He steps aside, ready to walk out.

The revolutions in my head gain speed. He is my relative.

He is our relative, family. Mama's voice echoes in the distance. He is the husband of my mother's younger sister's sister-in-law. I ask Mama what I should call him. Malume, she says.

They made a mistake with his surname. It's Mdladlane. I know. It's a mistake people make frequently because Dladla is a more common surname.

Presently Mapule speaks, causing the delegates to distribute another bout of silence.

'Comrades, can we all stand up, and in silence honour the fallen comrade.' We all rise. A yawning silence engulfs the room.

They got the surname wrong. They got the surname wrong. I become conscious again only when I hear '*Amandla*' and the response, '*Awethu*.'

The delegates sit.

'Comrades, is there anyone in this room who knows the fallen comrade? Can they please say a word or two about him?'

I feel a lump in my throat. It gets larger as my mind tries to guide me, 'talk, don't talk.' 'Talk.' 'Don't talk.' Another Kaunda silence. The veins in my head are beginning to throb.

Mapule continues, now facing comrade S'bu, 'On behalf of the conference delegates we'd like to thank you, comrade S'bu, for bringing us the news, sad though it is. I trust that I speak on behalf of everyone in this room today. We shall never surrender. We are all in here today taking the spear that Comrade Reverend has left. This conference is a testimony to that fact. *Amandla!*' Comrade S'bu lifts his right fist, firm. Then he slowly gets off the stage. He walks out of the room, using a side door close to the stage.

Like in a video, events unfold in my head. I'm back in 1977, twelve years ago. Mama is doing her motherly duty. She gives me the number and address. She informs me it will be a good church to go to. That I should be well behaved, visit the family, treat them as I would my own family. I must be helpful 'cause they may need me. She reminds me they have younger children and that I should be a sister to them, just as I am with my siblings. I am nineteen years old, leaving home for the big city, Pietermaritzburg, to train as a teacher.

'Comrade Mapule ...' a voice, accompanied by a hand in the air almost shouts from the back. She doesn't wait for a response. She walks through the chairs in no time, delegates watching. The chairperson waits, clearly giving her permission to speak. She stands in front, without getting onto the stage, speaks loudly without the microphone.

'Comrades, I am thoroughly disturbed by this news. I don't know Reverend Dladla, but as someone coming from Natal, the absence of anyone in this room who knows him is a clear demonstration of our movement's weaknesses.'

By now the silence pounds, I'm aware of its rhythm.

Images continue to unfold.

I called him Malume, just as Mama suggested. He started by making time when we could be alone. He would drive me to the hostel after I'd had supper at their home. He would insist I didn't take the taxi. Auntie would agree. On some days I cooked supper, as Auntie didn't enjoy spending prolonged periods in the kitchen. I was doing as Mama had instructed. I liked the children. I helped with homework. They liked me. They called me Sisi.

'The movement is failing the Zulus among us comrades. People are dying in Natal. Our people. What has the movement done, so far, *hhe*? Can anyone here and now say what the movement has done about the special case in Natal?'

I recognise her, immediately. We spoke at length when she came to the registration desk. Her complexion matches black olives. She is based in Moscow, is a medical doctor. I don't remember her name.

Malume always had a chocolate bar. He would let me step out of the car first then take a bar from his cubby-hole and say something like, 'Thank you. Your aunt's health is going down and down. She really appreciates your coming over to cook for us.' I would take the bar, thank him and disappear into the hostel. I didn't understand auntie's health problem. She seemed fine to me. Secretly I thought she was just lazy, the complaining type, a hypochondriac really.

I still wish to correct the small detail. He is Reverend Mdladlane. Such detail is important. I can't find my voice. It's too late anyway. The mood in the plenary room has changed. I should have spoken then, at that moment, when I was invited to speak. I decide to let it go.

'This is a special case that deserves the movement's attention. I cannot sit here and watch us observe a moment of silence and then continue as if nothing happened.' Comrade Moscow finishes talking and walks slowly, back to her seat.

The room begins to vibrate now, voices coming from all corners.

'I support the comrade who just spoke.'

Heads turn to where the half-shouting voice comes room. Someone from the centre of the room is speaking right where she is seated. Then everyone begins to talk at the same time.

Someone from the back, close to my team's table, starts shouting, her voice carries over every other voice. I don't remember seeing her face at all.

'Comrades, I'm based in Angola. As comrades from Natal we've been raising this issue with our commanders and commissars in the camps. We are soldiers, comrades. We want to be deployed back home to face the enemy. Our own people have now become our enemy. The state has turned them against us. We are soldiers. We can face Inkatha. What do our commanders and commissars say? 'Not yet, comrades. Comrades, that's not a good tactic. Comrades, our tactics need to match our strategy. Comrades, this is a very delicate matter. Comrades, we have to wait for ...'

'Order! Order comrades!' Mapule, speaks through the mike with a vehemence I never suspected she has. It dawns on me this is why she has the job of chairing.

The speed with which the action unfold make my head feel bigger.

One day, about six months down the line, as he drops me off he thanks me for having been helpful as Auntie had been sick for three weeks. He says he wants to thank me properly by doing something special.

Auntie had been in hospital for a week. For the first time I believed she was really ill. I had done the best I could to make her and the children comfortable. My schoolwork suffered that week. I was spending far too much time away from the hostel.

I tell him it was nothing. Auntie is like Mama to me. I did exactly what I would have done with Ma.

It takes time before the Kaunda room responds to the order plea.

Mapule waits for the silence to settle before she speaks.

'I know this is hard for us all comrades. I may not be from Natal but I know the pain the comrades must be feeling ...'

'It's time for action. Now,' a voice bellows from the left side of the room. It's a male comrade.

Mapule interjects 'Comrade, order! You have an observer status during this conference.'

'As I was saying, comrades,' Mapule starts again, 'The issue of escalating violence in Natal is undeniably critical. However, this conference is focused on something else. Something I know is close to all our hearts, a non-sexist constitution, a route to women's liberation.'

I'm already out of the car when he tells me about his idea. He asks if I've ever been to the Lion Park. I shake my head. He wants to take me there, on a Saturday when I don't have to worry about school. How generous, I think. Two of my friends had just been there, thanks to their boyfriends. They went there as a group, a foursome, for a picnic. They could not stop talking about the fun they had.

The doctor from Moscow stands to speak without permission from Mapule. 'Therein lies the problem, comrades. Are women not dying in the state sponsored, Inkatha-executed slaughter in Natal as we speak? Are women not victims of the state's violent machinery? Are women not dying, comrades? If we are here to discuss women's liberation, I say the current crisis in Natal deserves urgent attention from us. Us women, at this very conference.'

I like the way she speaks. I agree with her. It seems that most of the delegates feel as I do. Many are nodding and making agreeing sounds.

'*Amandla!*', a voice shouts from the front row.

'*Awethu!*' the Kaunda room reverberates.

Comrade Mapule takes the mike in her hand and talks.

'Comrades, this is a plea. Such events are meant to destabilise us. The enemy knows that such news will distract our focus. It's an old trick. Do something to derail the energies of the forces that are against you and you win. We cannot allow that to happen.'

Silence descends again.

On the Saturday we agreed upon Malume arrives alone at the hostel to pick me up. I ask about the kids. He says it will just be the two of us. My treat. It's his expression of gratitude.

There's something in the way he says that that makes me feel ill at ease.

My friends are waving me good-bye from the stairs in front of the car park. They wish me a groovy time and I relax.

Lion Park, here I come.

We take off.

Mapule continues, 'I have two suggestions. First and very important, let's remind ourselves that in this movement, we are one. There are no Zulus, Xhosas, Sothos, nothing. Dividing us along tribal lines was also a strategy for the Boers. Let's remember that as we move forward, comrades. This is not a theoretical suggestion. Thinking differently is an active process. My second suggestion is predicated on this mind shift. Secondly, I'd propose that we put the Natal issue ...'

'It's a crisis, comrades. A crisis.'

I know her. She works in the Youth League offices. Very tall for a woman, the long braids give her face a look of someone older. Names are hard to remember today with so many faces to work with. Her loud voice quivers.

'Unless we start thinking about it that way we will not give it the attention it deserves. We need a strategy that responds adequately to this crisis. Comrade Reverend's death is meant to remind us of that. It is not a coincidence.'

'Order, comrade.'

Mapule starts again.

'I suggest we add the Natal crisis to our agenda. This will mean extending the time. We already have a full agenda. We cannot cut it. So, comrades, we'll need to sacrifice. Stay on till late tonight. Let's plan to break for supper as stated on the agenda, take just one hour and get back at 8 PM sharp to focus on the Natal crisis.'

'Elethu!' I second comrade chair. '*Ama...ndla!*' doctor Moscow shouts.

The way she carries her black conference t-shirt and black trousers makes her pronouncements more believable. Maybe it's her sturdy body. Maybe it's the doctor in her. She has a presence, one that says 'take me seriously'.

'*Awethu!*'

I start to feel pins and needles in my legs. I rise from the squatting position I've been in, walk down the stage back to our admin table. Now I feel alone as I walk down the centre of all the delegates. By the time I get to the table and sit the room is silent again.

The scenery stretches ahead as we drive. The road between Pietermaritzburg and Durban has hillocks that rise and fall for kilometres and kilometres on end. I am half excited. Malume speaks a lot. He does not give me time to say much. He is talking about the family, then skips to his church work, then back to the family and the community he works with. Now and again he turns to look at me as if to see if I understand him. My eyes are fixed on the hillocks.

'I also second Comrade Mapule.'

It's Nomazwi, our team leader. She stood up without my noticing. She is now standing right at the centre, in the corridor next to our table. Heads turn to face her. She would pass as a hospital matron, a kind and sensible one. Yesterday she told me she is a social scientist, teaches at a university in Namibia. Her Afrikaans sounds like that of the Boers, back home. During our AST meetings she slips in and out of it.

'Mapule is making a good point, comrades. I suggest we do as she suggests. That way we stay focussed.'

She steps back to her seat.

Someone shouts, '*Ama...ndla!*'

'*Awethu!*'

'Thank you comrades, we will now proceed. Comrade Lungi, back to you.'

I notice the sign to the Lion Park and begin to look forward to the picnic. He turns into the park, pays at the gate and begins the slow drive into the enclosed wilderness.

When Lungi speaks again I look up and really listen. I realise that her voice has a husky ring to it that makes you want to listen. Even from the back of the room she looks distinct, the black and white kente cloth adds a layer of elegance to her frame.

'Thank you, comrade Mapule. In the interest of time comrades, I propose that I skip the first ... hm ... let me see. In the first section I was going to give you a broad outline, very broad, a brushstroke really, on the history of town planning world wide but zooming in on philosophies and theories of planning. Ok, I'll skip that section. My paper is in your files ...'

The Kaunda room begins to move. Delegates feel around for their files.

I am surprised the transformation is so much so close to the highway. The gravel road forces the car to slow down. I think it's even slower than the recommended speed. It's very dry. Trees look unhealthy, starved and sparse. There isn't much grass. I ask about the lions.

He turns, puts his left hand on my thigh, stares into my face, slowing the car down further. His left hand moves to the inner side of my thigh.

I freeze.

'Read that when you have time. I'll also skip the second section but suggest that you read that thoroughly because I delve into crucial issues: heritage, values, African values and design as they relate to town planning. That section gives you the context that will be useful when we look at liberation of blacks and women.'

He tells me that the lions are in their own enclosure, at the other end. That's where we will enjoy our picnic. The picnic spot is right in front of the lions.

The car stops. I look around, suspecting there's some wild life to admire.

Then everything happens so confusingly, so unexpectedly quickly, so violently.

Reverend Malume is all over me, his hands, his face. He is kissing me, breathing heavily, his hand is between my thighs, groping.

'The third section is on governance. I'll also skip that. It's an easy read. Hmm ... I'll start my detailed presentation with the fourth section, on spatial concepts. As I mentioned earlier when I outlined my presentation, I believe strongly that women's freedom cannot be separated from apparently benign issues like physical space.'

It feels as if the whole car is moving as he manages to throw me onto the back seat of the car. I don't know how and when he lowered the front seat. I see him, his changed face, as he keeps looking fiercer and fiercer.

His body is heavy on mine. He keeps lifting it off as he instructs me to undress while he unzips his trouser.

I cannot hear everything he says between his groans. All I can focus on is how to get from under his body and out of the car.

My left hand has found the door handle. I pray the car is not locked.

'So, comrades I want to start this section then by doing a short exercise. I hope the exercise will also get those of us whose eyes are closing to wake up.'

Some delegates laugh. Lungi smiles.

'I need you to sit in groups of five. Let's move quickly into groups then I will tell you what do to next.'

I see his penis, black and rod-like, shooting through.

I panic.

He moves off me. I see he needs room to undress properly.

I use this time to pull the handle down. It flings open.

With all my might, I push him away, wriggle, roll and throw myself onto the gravel. I do not believe I am out of the car.

I get up and run. I run into the wilderness.

I stay on the road. I pray for another car to appear.

When I turn back, there is a car. His.

'Are you in dreamland, comrade Zodwa?' Nomazwi pokes my arm with her forefinger and a smile. 'We don't have to move, there's five of us.' My team is looking at me. The whole room is abuzz as delegates rearrange themselves into groups.

I can't do this. I just know I cannot do this.

'Comrades please, you have to excuse me. I have to, I have to run, I mean, I have to go to the toilet.'

I don't wait to hear what they have to say. I stand up, push the door open and run out and away, to my room.

I run faster and faster as his car gets closer. The plan in my head is clear. I am running until there's another car in sight. The wild animals can do as they please. I want to see him and his Christian conscience watch me getting eaten up.

I run.

I run around buildings, not through their corridors. When I arrive at my block I take the stairs instead of the lift. I take some of them two at a time. I hold firmly onto the rail with each step. I stop only to catch my breath. I reach the fifth floor and turn left. My room is the second room after the stairs. I am grateful for having volunteered that it doubles up as an office. It seemed logical, for a runner. I share it with boxes, files, books, t-shirts, stationery. Everything the AST needed stored for the conference.

I look back. I notice another car approach. My plan will work. The road is so narrow cars cannot overtake. When the other car is right behind him I stop running. He pulls up next to me.

'Get in the car. Have you lost your mind, *Thixo mtanandini*!'

Panting I open the back door and get in. He drives on without another word. I look back.

The car behind us follows. There are three passengers.

He picks up speed, far more than the allowed maximum.

I sit on my bed.

Looking at conference paraphernalia I begin to sob.

By the time we drive past the lions' enclosure swirls of dust follow us. I can't see anything behind us. He drives through the main gate. We reach the highway. We face Pietermaritzburg again. I sigh.

I have an irrepressible urge to tidy up, rearrange things into piles and rows.

I begin with the t-shirts. I re-fold. I re-pack.

I cannot stop crying, but things have to be in order before I decide what to do next.

Biographical Notes

WILLEMIEN DE VILLIERS is an artist and writer. She has published two novels – *Kitchen Casualties* and *The Virgin in the Treehouse*, as well as several short stories published in various collections. She lives in with her family in Cape Town, at the start of Peck's Valley below Muizenberg Peak.

ALEXANDRA DODD is a writer and editor based in Johannesburg, where she is a regular contributor to *Wanted*, *Business Day Arts*, *Art South Africa*, *VISI* and others. She lectures in the writing programme at the University of the Witwatersrand, and edits fiction. She has also contributed texts to numerous publications on South African artists, including Marco Cianfanelli, Sam Nhlengethwa and David Goldblatt.

JOANNE FEDLER's books include *The Dreamcloth* and *Secret Mothers Business*. She lives in Sydney.

AMANDA GERSH attended the University of Cape Town and received an MFA from Columbia University in New York. Her writing has been published in such magazines as *Open City*, *One Story*, *Tin House* and *The Believer*. Amanda lives in Wyoming where she is at work on *The Disappearing House*, a collection of stories.

COLLEEN HIGGS is the Information Manager at the Centre for the Book in Cape Town, where she manages several projects, including the Community Publishing Project. She has published poetry and short fiction.

KIRSTEN MILLER is a writer from Durban, South Africa. She has published short stories and numerous articles, and currently contributes regularly to *Sawubona* magazine. She is the author of *Children on the Bridge* and *All is Fish*.

MUTHAL NAIDOO, a former playwright and retired teacher, now writes short stories.

HENRIETTA ROSE-INNES was born in 1971 in Cape Town. She has published two novels, *Shark's Egg* and *The Rock Alphabet*, and her short stories and essays have appeared in a variety of publications. In 2006 she edited a compilation entitled *Nice Times! A Book of South African Pleasures and Delights*. In 2007 she was a Fellow at the Akademie Schloss Solitude in Stuttgart. Henrietta Rose-Innes's story 'Poison' won the 2007 Southern African PEN / HSBC Award, and she was shortlisted for the 2007 Caine Prize for African Writing.

ANNE SCHUSTER lives in Cape Town. Her poetry and short stories are found in a number of collections, and she has written two novels. The latest, *Foolish Delusions*, was published in 2005, and is being translated into German. Anne conducts writing workshops for individuals and organisations, and works with groups of women – such as women on farms, women in prisons and refugees – enabling them to write and publish their stories.

MARY WATSON SEOGHIE lives in Cape Town. Her collection of interlinking stories, *Moss*, was published in 2004. She is currently lecturing in Film Studies at the University of Cape Town where she received a meritorious publication award for *Moss*. She was awarded the Caine Prize in 2006. She has contributed several short stories to published anthologies, including translations in Afrikaans, German, Italian and Dutch.

MAKHOSAZANA XABA is the author of *These Hands*, a volume of poetry that is currently undergoing translation into French. She holds an MA in Creative Writing (cum laude) from the University of the Witwatersrand. 'Running' won the 2005 Deon Hofmeyr Award for Creative Writing. She was awarded a year long Writing Fellowship by the Wits Institute for Social and Economic Research (WISER), during which she worked on a biography project.

Acknowledgements

These stories are, in the main, new stories. However Anne Schuster's *In a State of Emergency* first appeared in SASH Magazine, volume 30 no.2, August 1987. *Coming in to Land*, by Willemien de Villiers appeared in Women Flashing, edited by Anne Schuster, 2006. *Running*, by Makhosazana Xaba, won the 2005 Deon Hofmeyr Award for Creative Writing.